D1525477

Yoga Can Be Fatal – A Senior Sleuthing Club Cozy Mystery – Book 3

by

Jinty James

Yoga Can Be Fatal – A Senior Sleuthing Club Cozy Mystery – Book 3

by

Jinty James

Copyright © 2023 by Jinty James

ISBN:9798867514792

DEDICATION

To the real Teddy, my wonderful
Mother, Annie, and AJ.

CHAPTER 1

"Are you going to twist yourself into a pretzel at this yoga class?" Martha asked.

"I hope not," Pru answered her roommate and friend.

"Ruff?" Teddy, the nine-month-old white Coton de Tulear, peered at Pru, his fur springing up under his eyes.

It was late Tuesday afternoon in April, and Pru had just gotten home from her job as assistant librarian. She just had time to grab her yoga gear and head to the new class being held in the small town of Gold Leaf Valley.

"Are you sure you don't want to come?" she asked Martha.

"Nope." Martha's short gray curls sprung around her surprisingly youthful face as she shook her head. "Just getting around with this thing—" she patted her rolling walker "—is enough exercise for me. Most of the time, anyway."

"You mean when you're not chasing down suspects?" she gently teased.

"That's right." Martha nodded vigorously.

"Ruff!"

"After all, I am president of our senior sleuthing club," Martha continued with a grin. "If I don't take down the bad guys, who will?"

"The police?"

"That's if we don't catch them first." Martha sounded just like Pru imagined the fictional retired lady detective would, in the TV script Martha had been working on for a while now.

"You go off and enjoy yourself," Martha said. "When you get home, we can order pizza for dinner – and it's my turn to choose."

"True." Pru smiled at them and hurried out the door. When she'd arrived in the Gold-Rush era town last year, her housing options had been limited to the local motel – until she'd heard that Martha needed a roommate. The situation had suited them both, as well as Teddy, and now the three of them were firm friends.

She hopped into her silver SUV, slinging her yoga mat and blanket into the passenger seat. When a woman had put up a poster at the library advertising classes, Pru had been intrigued. It had been a while since she'd taken a yoga class, and she hadn't kept up with her home practice. Today was the perfect time to start anew.

After driving a few blocks, she arrived at the small studio on the main street and climbed up the flight of stairs. Wooden handrails lined each side of the staircase. Below was a small accountant's office, with a sign saying they were closed for a two-week vacation.

Opening the wooden door, Pru, wearing black yoga pants and a blue T-shirt, stepped inside the studio. She almost tripped over a small nail lying on the ground near the doorway. Glancing up, she took notice of the big, bare room, with wooden floorboards and small windows. Five ladies were already sitting cross-legged on their mats, including her friend Zoe, from the Norwegian Forest Cat Café.

"Over here!" The slim, twenty-something girl patted the empty space next to her, her brunette pixie cut highlighting her features. "That's Sunny." She jerked her head toward an athletic woman wearing khaki yoga pants and matching crop top, sitting cross-legged facing the others.

"Thanks." Pru settled down next to her in the front row, looking around curiously. Their instructor was busy checking her phone, her copper brown hair cut in a short, flattering style with a layered fringe sweeping across her forehead. She had an air of efficiency about her. The other students murmured to each other.

"Am I late?" Doris, another friend of Pru's, rushed in and looked around. She wore wrinkled jeans,

4

and a red and white checked shirt, her short hair looking a little messy.

"Jeans are not acceptable." Sunny looked up and frowned at Doris. "Proper yoga outfits only."

"Oh – I'm sorry." Doris flushed and looked down at the tote bag in her hand where an old red blanket peeked out, along with a black yoga mat.

"It will have to do for today," Sunny said in annoyance, "but don't bother coming back next week if you can't dress appropriately."

There was a small, collective gasp, including Pru's. She looked up at Doris and patted the empty space next to her. Doris sank down next to her and took off her shoes, her head down.

"Shoes at the door," Sunny barked.

"Yeah, shoes at the door," a girl with ash-blonde hair in a tight ponytail said. She wore a silver nose-ring and her eyebrows looked professionally sculpted. "Everyone knows *that*."

"Not if they're new to yoga," Pru replied.

"Yeah," Zoe chimed in. "How would someone know if they're not told?"

"They're told now," Sunny snapped, glancing at the girl who had spoken. "Is anyone else coming, Danielle?"

"Not that I know of." Danielle frowned. "I told everyone at the Sacramento studio about this class and how awesome it was going to be – much better than anything Angela has. And everyone promised to come."

Sunny glanced at her sports watch. "We might as well start now. My classes do *not* run late." She looked at Doris. "You – what's your name?"

"Doris." Doris gulped and flushed.

"Sit cross-legged like the others."

"Okay." Doris wriggled herself into position, a little "ouch" escaping from her lips.

"First, we will warm up our necks." Sunny demonstrated, slowly moving her head to the left, and then back to the right. "Five sides each. And then we will—"

The door burst open and a tall man with dark hair strode across the room. "I told you I needed the rent paid on time." He scowled at Sunny.

Pru's eyes widened and she looked first at Zoe on her left, and then at Doris on her right. They each looked just as taken aback as she did.

"Not now, Kevin," Sunny snapped. "I'm teaching a class."

"I made it clear when you leased this space that you needed to pay the rent up front."

"And I will," Sunny replied. "Tonight. I told you, there was a mix up at the bank and my payment didn't go through. Why don't you storm into the bank and demand they give you my rent money instead of disrupting my class like this?"

"Not much of a class," he sneered, his gaze sweeping the seven students.

"Next week's will be twice as big," Sunny told him. "Now get out of here!"

"That rent better be paid tonight." He gave her a black look.

From her vantage point, Pru couldn't help a shiver. The expression on Kevin's face chilled her spine.

He stalked out of the room, slamming the door shut behind him.

There was a small silence.

"Necks," Sunny spoke. "Five movements each side. Let's go, people!"

"It's just as well Lauren didn't come," Zoe whispered out of the side of her mouth to Pru as she mentioned her cousin and colleague at the cafe. "She wouldn't like this."

"I don't know if I like it so far," she admitted in a hushed tone of her own. Still, she wanted to be fair, and the class had only started five minutes ago.

"Am I doing it right?" Doris asked Pru anxiously, turning her head to the left.

She glanced up at Sunny who sat in front of them, moving her neck while staring at her phone screen. Was she checking on the bank payment mix-up? Or something else?

"It looks right to me," Pru replied reassuringly.

"Thanks." Doris gave a little smile.

"No talking!" Danielle raised her voice. "Sunny, they're talking!"

"Anyone who talks again will be sent to the back row. I won't tell you again, people. You're here to do yoga, not talk!"

Danielle smirked at Doris, then returned her admiring gaze to Sunny, who put her phone down and focused on the students.

"Get ready for sphinx," Sunny barked. She lay on her stomach and rested on her elbows, looking like the famous Egyptian statue. "Sphinx, not cobra, everyone! You, Doris, what are you doing?"

Pru peeked at her friend, who was struggling to push herself up on her arms.

"I don't know," Doris replied miserably. "I've never done yoga before."

"You've never done …" Sunny clapped a hand to her forehead, otherwise maintaining her impeccable sphinx pose.

"The poster in the library didn't say beginners weren't welcome," Pru found her voice.

"That's right!" Zoe agreed. "I'm a beginner, too."

"But you're a lot better than *her*." Sunny pointed at Doris.

"Only people who *deserve* to do yoga are allowed in Sunny's class," Danielle told them loftily.

"The ad said everyone welcome." Pru frowned.

"Hush, Danielle," Sunny admonished her. Glancing at Doris, she said, "Copy her," and pointed to Pru.

After doing sphinx, then cobra, they moved into downward dog.

"Yuck," Zoe panted, her palms and the balls of her feet on the mat. "I thought my fitness wasn't bad, but …"

"I know," Pru sympathized. She was feeling her lack of practice, her arms straining to maintain the posture.

"Help!" Doris crumpled into a heap on the floor.

Sunny tsked, but otherwise ignored her.

"Are you okay?" Pru murmured.

"I think so." Doris raised her head to face her. "I came straight here from an eight-hour shift at Gary's. Maybe I should have tried this on my day off."

"Hey, want to grab a burger there when class is finished?" Zoe suggested, looking at both of them sideways.

"I'd love to," Pru replied, "but Martha is waiting at home for me. We're going to order pizza."

"Ooh – yum!" Zoe's eyes lit up, while her head still faced down. "That's a good idea. I think I'll do that too when I get home. How about next week? The three of us could go to

Gary's after this—" she dropped her voice even more "—torture session is over."

"That sounds great." Pru smiled. "How about you, Doris?"

"If I live that long," Doris joked. "But it sounds good. I can use my discount for us."

"Awesome!"

"You!" Sunny pointed at Zoe. "Back row – now!"

"Oops." Zoe stood and mimed zipping her lips shut. "Sorry."

Pru turned to look at her as Zoe moved to the empty back row, unable to help smiling when Zoe winked at her.

"Stand," Sunny ordered. "Get into warrior one."

"What's warrior …" Doris's voice trailed off as the door opened with a bang.

Pru turned to look at the newcomer, and then wished she hadn't. It was her worst nightmare come true.

CHAPTER 2

"Am I late?" the newcomer asked, her tone not seeming to care if she was or not. She was around Pru's age, mid-twenties, and wore her light caramel hair in waves cascading over her shoulders. Her outfit of gold yoga pants and black, long-sleeved top criss-crossing at the back showed off her slim figure.

"Yes," Sunny growled. "Back row."

"Pru!" The girl smiled. "I hoped you'd be here. When I saw the poster at the motel, I wondered if you'd attend."

"Bridget," she managed to get out evenly.

"No more talk!" Sunny clapped her hands once. "The next person who speaks will be thrown out, and you will *not* get a refund!"

"Yeah!" Danielle murmured, then became silent when Sunny's frown turned on her.

Pru couldn't concentrate on the rest of the class. What was Bridget doing here? How did she know that Pru lived here now? And why on earth had she hoped that Pru would be at this class?

Sunny barked at her a few times, criticizing her posture, but she didn't care. All Pru could think about was why Bridget was in town.

Finally, the class ended with a scant three-minute relaxation in corpse pose.

"I expect to see everyone back here the same time next week," Sunny informed them when everyone started rolling up their mats. "And tell your friends."

"Yeah, tell your friends," Danielle parroted.

Sunny glanced at her. "That reminds me, Danielle, when are you starting your teacher training?"

"The course was full so I couldn't enroll," the girl explained. "I've put my name down on the waitlist in case anyone drops out."

"They probably won't," Sunny replied. "That course is renowned for the quality of its new yoga teachers. You've been talking about teaching for a while now – when are you actually going to do it?"

"Soon," Danielle mumbled.

"Sunny!" The door banged open and a tall woman with raven hair stormed in. She wore black yoga pants, a white T-shirt, and a thunderous expression on her face.

"Angela," Sunny greeted her with a smirk.

"Don't you dare steal my students!" The woman stalked to the front of the room and poked her finger in Sunny's khaki-clad chest. "You've worked for me for how long? I paid you well, made allowances for your teaching style because somehow several students seemed to like your classes, but this is how you repay me?"

"What did you expect me to do?" Sunny shrugged. "You wouldn't give me a raise, or schedule the classes to suit me. Of course I was going to walk."

"But poaching my students …" Angela fisted her hands on her hips. "That's a new low, even for you."

"Can I help it if they prefer my rigorous style over your insipid one?" Sunny asked. "It's a free country, isn't it? People can join whichever yoga class they want."

"Yeah," Danielle added.

Both instructors turned and scowled at her.

"People need to be pushed to their physical best," Sunny continued. "My classes do that. And you know students can't get enough of it."

"*Some* students." Angela shook her head. "I think you've done me a favor. Your quitting saved me the paperwork of firing you. And if any students at my center want to join your classes—" she swept her gaze over the attendees, one of whom blushed "—then good luck to you. May you enjoy the yoga you deserve." She stalked out of the room.

"Wow!" Zoe rushed over to Pru. "I wonder what that was all about?"

"You probably wouldn't understand, because you haven't been to Angela's studio." Danielle joined them, her fancy yoga mat under her arm, and holding a pair of pristine white sneakers. "Angela's been holding back Sunny for years – now Sunny can strike out on her own and totally dominate the yoga world."

"Pru." Bridget came up to her.

She'd almost forgotten about her due to the drama she'd just witnessed.

"Yes?" She stared at her ex-best friend, wondering what she'd ever seen in her. By now, Pru knew not to be fooled by her charming exterior.

"I thought we could grab a bite to eat after class and catch up." Bridget had a puzzled look on her face, as if she wasn't expecting Pru's aloof manner.

"Sorry, I'm expected home."

"She's already got a dinner date." Zoe winked at Pru.

"You're seeing someone?" Bridget sounded surprised.

"Yep, she's definitely seeing someone tonight," Zoe said in a cheery tone.

"Well … see you around." Bridget picked up her yoga mat and walked slowly out of the room.

Not if I see you first.

"Sorry, I shouldn't have interfered," Zoe said after a moment. "But I noticed how shocked you looked when she came into class and joined me in the back row. I shouldn't have meddled, though."

"I'm glad you did," Pru replied with a smile.

"Do you know her well?" Doris asked, stuffing her yoga mat and blanket into her bag.

"I thought I did – last year. It's a long story." And not one she felt like explaining right now.

"You know I'm here if you ever feel like talking," Zoe said. "Lauren, too. And Annie. She might be a Norwegian Forest Cat but she's a great listener and loves helping when she can."

"I know." Pru nodded.

"That goes for me, too," Doris said.

"Thanks." Pru smiled at her new friends. "And I've got Martha and Teddy as well. I think I'm very lucky I ended up here in Gold Leaf Valley. Maybe Bridget actually did me a favor."

"Are you coming to yoga next week?" Zoe's eyes glinted with mischief as they walked out the door, leaving Sunny talking to a couple of students, including Danielle.

"I'm not." Doris shook her head. "My legs are so wobbly, I'm not sure if I can make it to my car and it's parked right outside."

"I know what you mean," Pru sympathized. "Unfortunately, I think this yoga class was a mistake." *In more ways than one.*

CHAPTER 3

"You mean that girl who hung you out to dry after she used you to cheat on her exams turned up at yoga class?" Martha wanted to know.

"Yes." Pru ate another slice of pepperoni and mushroom pizza in Martha's kitchen. Right now, the comfort food was doing its job.

"Ruff!" Teddy added in indignation. He'd been begging for table scraps, but they hadn't given in to temptation as pepperoni wasn't recommended for dogs.

"She's got a nerve," Martha tsked. "What on earth is she doing here? She's from Colorado, same as you, right?"

"That's right."

"Huh. Well, she'd better not turn up here, otherwise she'll feel the business-end of my walker."

"Ruff!" *Yes!*

"Thanks." She couldn't help smiling at both of them. "I have no idea why she's in town and I didn't want to ask. All I know is she's staying at the motel which is where she saw the flyer for the yoga class."

"It's just as well I didn't come with you tonight. There's no way I could have done all those exercises – poses," Martha corrected herself. "And I've never heard of this Sunny." She frowned. "Or this Angela. But if they're from Sacramento, then it's no wonder. But why someone from there would want to drive an hour to Gold Leaf Valley to set up a yoga class, I have no idea."

"Nor me. Maybe she thought she'd draw a big crowd since she's the only yoga teacher here?"

"Could be." Martha nodded. "Kevin, I've heard of. He owns a couple of little stores on the main street. But I never thought he was the type to let someone rent from him without paying upfront."

After dinner, Pru flopped down in front of the TV. Although she tried to concentrate on the mystery drama, her thoughts kept drifting to Bridget.

Why was she really here? She'd thought they were best friends in college – until Bridget had shown her true colors. Pru had nearly gotten kicked out of school. Bridget had left, and she'd never heard from her again. She assumed Bridget had been expelled, but she didn't know for sure, as the whole matter had been hushed up as much as possible – then.

Hopefully Bridget would leave town ASAP – maybe even tomorrow. She held onto that thought as she finally drifted off to sleep.

***

The next day, Pru arrived at the library, determined not to think about Bridget.

Her boss, Barbara, was at the reference desk helping a patron find out about the types of cheese in eighteenth century France.

Pru pushed the cart of returned books to the Ds and started putting them away in order. She almost tsked when she saw a novel with the author's surname starting with Do in the Da section.

"Pru!"

She whirled around, her eyes widening at the sight of Bridget, dressed in blue jeans and a green T-shirt.

"What are you doing here?" Her breath caught in her throat.

"Looking for you." Bridget smiled.

"How did you know I worked here?"

"Oh, you know. Word gets around. Your mom told someone who told my mom. I've been travelling around, and thought I'd stop by and see you. But I didn't expect you to end up in such a dinky little town." She scrunched up her face. "I thought you'd get a librarian job in LA or San Franciso – even New York. Your grades were so good."

"They were," she acknowledged. "I guess that's why you used me to cheat."

"Oh, Pru, don't be like that." Bridget tossed back her head, her caramel waves cascading around her shoulders. "It was no biggie. Everyone does it."

Pru stared at her. *Everyone does it?*

"No, they don't," she managed. "And first of all, this is not a dinky little town. It's a great place. I was lucky to get a job at this library." She glanced around, remembering where they were, and lowered her voice. Luckily, there weren't any patrons nearby. "And secondly, I was nearly expelled from college."

"I *was*," Bridget admitted. "I didn't think they were going to do it. I wasn't the first person to try something like that, and they knew it. But I guess they decided to make an example out of me. Anyway, I'll have to get a job sometime, and thought you could put a word in for me here."

"What?" Pru blinked.

"It'll be great. We can hang out together again, just like we did in school."

"You mean, when you weren't partying instead of studying?"

"Okay, maybe I shouldn't have partied so hard," Bridget admitted. "That's why I had to – you know – so I could graduate. I didn't have time to study for the final exams. My grades were okay until then, though." When Pru didn't say anything, she continued, "I wasn't flunking out of the course until …"

Pru remained silent.

"So, I should be able to get a job here," Bridget informed her. "I bet they're desperate for librarians – I mean, who would want to work in this place?" She glanced around the shelves of books. "There's hardly anyone in here, anyway. I bet they're bored with all these books– they definitely need some new blood to choose the novels and hook a younger crowd."

"You wouldn't be assigned that task, even if you did get a job here," Pru told her, thinking there was no way on earth that Bridget stood a chance, even if the library was hiring, which it wasn't. After applying for countless assistant librarian positions, this was the only library that had interviewed her, and she was grateful when she'd received an offer. She'd found out recently that news of the cheating scandal had spread to prospective employers, which was why she'd encountered so many rejections. Why would Bridget think she could snag a job with no degree *and* a murky college background?

"You never know." Bridget winked. "I can be pretty persuasive."

"Not here," Pru told her. Her no-nonsense boss wouldn't fall for Bridget's – whatever it was. Now, she wondered how *she* could have fallen for it. At one stage, she'd thought Bridget was her best friend. Since the cheating scandal, she'd viewed her friend through new eyes – and didn't like what she saw.

"Pru." Barbara suddenly appeared. She wore a severe black business suit, and had walked so quietly on the carpeted floor that Pru hadn't been aware of her approach.

"Hi, I'm a friend of Pru's." Bridget stuck out her hand and smiled.

Barbara ignored the gesture.

"I need you to shelve those books before your lunchbreak." Barbara eyed the stack of books on the cart, and then the half full shelves. "You know how I feel about personal conversations in the library. Have them on your own time."

"Yes, Barbara," Pru murmured, aware that her boss only approved of hushed tones in the library as well. "I'm sorry." She felt resentful that she was the one who had to apologize. But she needed this job.

Barbara nodded, the sharp edges of her bob hitting her cheeks, and strode quietly back to the reference desk.

"You'll have to go," Pru told Bridget. "I've got work to do." She picked up a mystery novel and shelved it correctly in the Das.

"Okay." Bridget sounded a little surprised at Pru's assertive behavior. "I'll catch you later."

"Not here." Pru kept her gaze on the bookshelf.

"I'll see you at yoga next week. Or maybe even sooner. If I don't get bored before then."

She heartily wished that Bridget would get bored *right now*.

CHAPTER 4

Pru fumed for the rest of the day. In Gold Leaf Valley, only Martha and Teddy knew about her past, and she preferred to keep it that way. Even though she'd been found innocent in the cheating scandal, she'd still been tainted by association, and she was worried about how her new friends might react if she told them.

She'd wondered if one day she would confide in Jesse, the new police detective, but she didn't know exactly what they were to each other. Acquaintances? Semi-friends? Semi-flirty-friends? Martha was trying to push them together, but Pru wasn't sure if she wanted to date him – but then, she wasn't sure if she wanted to *not* date him. The whole Jesse thing was confusing.

She'd settled in Gold Leaf Valley, was making new friends, and now Bridget had to come along to … what? Ruin her new life? Or was

Bridget so oblivious to anything except herself that she didn't realize how much of an impact her presence was having on Pru? Probably the latter, she thought with a grimace.

When she arrived home, her spirits lifted when Teddy greeted her at the door, his tail wagging overtime.

"Ruff!" He smiled, showing little white teeth.

"I missed you." She bent to stroke him. "Did you play in the yard with Martha today?"

"Yes, he did." Martha trundled along the hall, wearing a turquoise jogging suit which matched Teddy's collar. "He brought the ball back every time, didn't you, little guy?"

"Ruff!"

"Would you like to go for a walk with me?" Pru asked.

"Ruff!" *Yes!* Teddy stood on his hind legs.

"That would be good for him," Martha said. "I don't want his lead to get tangled up in my walker wheels."

"No problem." It would be nice to walk in the fresh air with a friend –

and she counted Teddy among her new friends.

"It's my turn to cook tonight," Martha announced, "and I'm making ribs with barbecue sauce. Out of that library book I borrowed a while ago and wrote down the recipe. So make sure you come back hungry." She chuckled.

Her mouth watered at the thought. They took turns to make dinner, and this rib recipe was delicious. Martha had made it before.

"I will," she assured her.

"Maybe I should get organized and invite Jesse over for dinner one night," Martha continued, "and make these ribs for him. I bet he'd definitely say yes if he knew they were on the menu."

"Martha," she began.

"Yeah, I know." Martha sighed gustily. "I shouldn't try to push you two together so hard. I haven't nagged you to wear your lipstick lately, have I?"

"No," she acknowledged.

"See?" Martha grinned.

Pru fetched Teddy's lead, and after she waved goodbye, they set out down the sidewalk. Victorian-era houses lined both sides of the street, as well as a few faux ones, such as Martha's yellow and cream duplex. Teddy sniffed at blades of grass, a bush, and a faint crack in the sidewalk as they ambled along in the late afternoon sunlight.

"Ruff!" Teddy suddenly towed her down the street.

She smiled when she saw a large, fluffy, silver-gray tabby walking sedately on a lavender harness held by a curvy girl with light brown hair with hints of gold.

"Hi, Lauren. Hi, Annie."

"Ruff!" Teddy greeted the cat, who responded with a "Brrt." They touched noses, their heads close together, as if communicating silently.

"Hi, Pru." Lauren glanced down at the two fur babies. "I'm sure they're having a private conversation."

"I think you're right." Pru laughed.

"Zoe told me about yoga class yesterday," Lauren continued. "I'm glad I didn't go – I don't think I would have lasted the whole session."

"Is Zoe attending next week?"

"She's undecided at the moment, which is unlike her." Lauren smiled wryly. "I think she's interested in yoga, but not that instructor."

"I know what she means." Pru shuddered. "Poor Doris – I thought it was great she came to try it out, but Sunny was quite rude to her."

"I definitely won't attend next week then," Lauren replied. "Oh – Father Mike came into the café the other day and mentioned Teddy had lent Mrs. Snuggle a toy a while ago. Annie wanted to do the same, so she fetched her toy hedgehog to give to her. That made me wonder – should we try a toy exchange for the three of them?"

"Ruff!" *Yes!* Teddy wagged his tail, his mouth wide in a smile.

"Brrt!" *Yes!*

"It looks like you got your answer." Pru nodded.

"Great." Lauren smiled. "What about Annie lending Teddy something?"

"Or Teddy could lend Annie one of his playthings."

"I'm sure Mrs. Snuggle has some toys – maybe we should ask Father Mike if she would be willing to part with any for a short period of time."

Father Mike had adopted a white Persian, a former show cat, a while ago, and although Mrs. Snuggle had a grumpy disposition, his kindness and goodness had won her over, and she was now devoted to him.

"I think it's a great idea," Pru remarked.

"I'll talk to Father Mike and see what he says," Lauren promised. "I'll update you when you come into the café – if not before."

"If Martha had her way, we'd be there every day." Pru laughed. "But by the time I get home from the library, it's too late."

"I understand." Lauren nodded. "Well, there's always Saturday morning."

"I can't wait!" Her mouth watered at the thought of the delicious cupcakes Lauren baked every day.

"Ruff!"

***

The next day, after she'd finished her shift at the library, Martha, Teddy, and Pru strolled down the main street.

"If we're quick, we can get to the handmade shop before it closes," Martha said. "I want to get some new fabric to make Teddy another bandana."

"Ruff!" Teddy's brown button eyes shone, and he wagged his tail.

"How many bandanas does he have now?" Pru asked.

"Lemme see." Martha screwed up her forehead in thought. "The one with the teddy bears on it, the scarlet ones, and another one I made last week from some old material I found at the bottom of my closet. But that was boring brown, and I don't think it suited him at all."

"And you don't have a brown outfit to match it," Pru guessed.

"That's right." Martha nodded. "I like wearing bright colors and I bet Teddy does, too – or at least interesting colors and not boring brown."

"Ms. Tobin wears a lot of brown sometimes," Pru mentioned Martha's friend.

"But it suits her now," Martha said. "A few years ago she wore dull old brown, but then she lightened up her wardrobe and now the brown tones she wears are nice and flatter her."

"What about my clothes?" Pru looked down at her tailored beige slacks and light green blouse. She hadn't changed her work clothes when she arrived home.

"They could do with a bit of jazzing up," Martha perused her thoughtfully. "That's why I keep telling you to wear your lipstick. But never mind, Jesse seems to like you just the way you are, and that's a good thing. Just think of how much money you'll save over the years if you don't buy makeup!"

Pru shook her head at Martha's reasoning. Spying the door of the yoga studio, she pointed it out to Martha. "That's where the yoga class was held."

"The door's open." Martha frowned. "Is class on again now?"

"Not that I know of." Pru stepped forward.

"Ruff!" Teddy nosed around the bottom of the door, and pushed his head against it. The door swung inward. "Ruff!"

"Teddy …" Pru's voice trailed off. Sunny was sprawled at the foot of the stairs, her eyes staring lifelessly at the ceiling.

CHAPTER 5

"Who is she?" Martha gripped the handles of her rolling walker, peering through the open door.

"Sunny. And it looks like she broke her neck on the stairs." She shuddered at the sight.

"We'd better call Mitch." Martha referred to Lauren's husband, who was the head detective in the town.

Pru noticed her friend's hand trembling when she reached for her phone buried in her walker basket.

"Let me," she said gently, conscious of a little wobble in her voice.

"Ruff?" Teddy stared at Sunny's body.

"We've gotta call the police." Martha sank down on her walker seat and stroked the small dog.

Pru fished her phone out of her purse and dialed.

"He said to wait here and not touch anything."

"Yuck. But you'd think we'd be used to dead bodies by now." Martha rallied. "This is our third."

"Unfortunately."

"Wuff," Teddy added in a little voice.

She tried to avoid looking at Sunny – the yoga instructor was definitely dead. Her gaze drifted up the staircase and then sharpened.

"Martha – does that look like a piece of wire along one of the upper steps?"

"Where?" Martha craned her head and squinted. "Oh yeah – I can make it out slightly. Make sure you tell Mitch."

"I will."

"Now we know why Sunny is dead down here." Martha pointed to the athletic woman's prone body. "Someone deliberately strung trip wire up there to kill her!"

***

"It's trip wire," Mitch confirmed a little later. Tall and good-looking, his hair was short and dark, and his brown eyes looked serious. He wore slate gray slacks and a white button-down shirt, with a matching gray jacket. "You went to the yoga class on Tuesday here, right?"

"Yes," Pru confirmed.

"Zoe told Lauren all about it, and Lauren told me. Sunny doesn't sound as if she was a popular instructor."

"There was one girl in the class who thought she was awesome." Pru thought back to Danielle's sycophantic attitude toward the instructor.

"Who else was in the class?"

"Doris, me, Zoe, Danielle who seemed to be a fan – I'm afraid I don't know the other ladies' names. A woman called Angela who used to work with Sunny in Sacramento came in at the end complaining about Sunny poaching her students, and a Kevin someone was there at the beginning asking for the rent."

"Don't forget your ex-best friend who cheated in college with *your* answers," Martha added. At Mitch's inquiring look, she added, "Oops. Sorry, Pru."

"You're right, Bridget was there." She took a deep breath and turned to Mitch. "I'm trying to put that behind me. Nobody knows about it in Gold Leaf Valley apart from Martha and Teddy."

"I understand," he replied quietly.

"She was totally innocent," Martha said. "It's that other gal you gotta watch out for. Fancy doing something like that to a sweet person like Pru. And now she has the nerve to show up here and—"

"I get the picture," Mitch assured her, then looked at Pru. "Do you know where I can find this ex-friend of yours?"

"Bridget said she was staying at the local motel," Pru replied.

"She should be easy to find, then." Mitch made a note. "Thanks. You three better go home now."

"The handmade shop is probably closed. We were going to buy some more fabric for Teddy's new bandana." Martha almost pouted.

"I'm sure you can do that tomorrow," Mitch said gently. "Did you drive over?"

"We walked," Martha said proudly. "Since my doctor keeps telling me I need to exercise more."

"I'll get a car to drive you home," Mitch said.

"Thanks." Pru gave him a small smile.

Mitch summoned a uniformed officer, and a few minutes later they arrived back at the duplex.

"Thank you," Pru said gratefully.

"Ruff!"

The young officer grinned when he looked at Teddy. "I've never seen a dog like that before. He's cute, that's for sure."

"And his fur feels like soft cotton wool," Martha said proudly. "That's why they named this breed a Coton."

Pru kept an eye on Martha as she slowly trundled into the house, instead of her usual racing car speed.

"I think I need a hot chocolate after all that." Martha sank into the yellow sofa, her walker parked next to her. Teddy hopped up on the seat and rested his head on her lap.

"I think Teddy needs a treat, too," Pru said.

"Ruff!" His ears pricked up at the word, then he settled down again.

"Good idea." Martha nodded.

Pru quickly made up the hot chocolate mix, then grabbed a dog cookie from the jar.

"Here you go." She held out the treat to the Coton, who took it nicely from her.

"Wuff," he said in a muffled tone, crunching on the liver and pumpkin cookie.

"You're welcome." She smiled at him, then gave Martha her mug.

"Thanks." Martha wrapped her hands around the mug. "I'm sure I'll feel better after this. And then we can have a senior sleuthing club meeting. We've gotta find out who killed Sunny!"

***

After they were fortified with hot chocolate, Martha declared the next meeting of the senior sleuthing club was now open.

"I think we should leave this matter to the police," Pru stated. "I'm sure Mitch will find the killer."

"Yeah, Mitch is good," Martha agreed. "But sometimes it takes him a little too long to find out who the murderer is."

"I guess because he's making sure he has enough evidence to back up an arrest."

"Probably." Martha nodded. "But it doesn't mean we can't help him catch Sunny's killer. Now, who would want her dead?"

"Everyone?" Pru asked wryly.

"It sounds like it. I think we should start with that yoga class you took. There's you, Zoe, your ex-best friend—"

"I hope you're not including me and Zoe as suspects," Pru said half joking, half serious.

"Of course *you're* not," Martha said. "And Zoe wouldn't do anything like that." She paused. "I don't think."

When Pru's eyes widened slightly, Martha added, "I like Zoe. She's a hoot. And she's a good girl. And she loves sleuthing just like me and Annie."

"Ruff?" Teddy looked up hopefully at Martha.

"And you, little guy." Martha chuckled, stroking him. "Okay, cross Zoe off our list."

"We haven't actually written anything down yet," Pru pointed out.

"Grab a piece of paper then," Martha directed good-naturedly.

She picked up a notepad from the coffee table, along with a half-chewed pen, courtesy, she suspected, of Teddy.

"Write this down," Martha instructed. "We've got Kevin, the landlord, that Angela lady who accused Sunny of stealing her students, your ex-best friend." She pursed her mouth in thought. "Who else?"

"The other students," Pru replied. "But I don't know who they are."

"Just write down other students. Doris!" Martha pointed her finger at her.

"I'm sure Doris wouldn't kill anyone," Pru protested.

"And she does work at Gary's Burger Diner, so knows how to cook a good hamburger." Martha nodded. "Those are two points in her favor."

"How about she seems like a nice person as well?"

"That's a good point, too. But sometimes the people we like turn out to be killers. Okay, put a question mark next to her name."

Pru did so reluctantly, wanting to cross out her friend's name altogether.

"Danielle," she suddenly blurted. "The girl who thought Sunny was a great instructor."

"Yeah!" Martha watched her write down the name. "Well, that gives us plenty to go on for the moment. Tomorrow we can start questioning them."

"I have to go to work tomorrow," Pru said.

"Pooh." Martha screwed up her face. "I guess we can start sleuthing when you get home. Just don't be late!"

CHAPTER 6

"Pru, dear, has my new book arrived yet?"

She glanced up from the library computer to find Ms. Tobin looking at her with an inquiring expression on her face.

"I don't remember it coming in," she told the middle-aged woman, who was dressed in an amber skirt and short-sleeved cream blouse. Tall and slim, the outfit suited her, and her brown hair. "Let me check."

After looking up Ms. Tobin's details, she shook her head. "No," she apologized.

"I've already browsed the shelf where the reserves are held and it's not there, either." Ms. Tobin frowned. "What a shame. I was really looking forward to reading it this afternoon."

"I'm sorry," she replied. "I could call you when it comes in if you like?"

"That would be nice," Ms. Tobin replied. "Thank you. I was at the café just now and heard about your yoga instructor being murdered."

"Already?" Pru's eyes widened.

"Word spreads quickly in such a small town. I overheard Lauren tell Zoe, since she took the yoga class with you."

"She did."

"And that you and Martha found the body."

"And Teddy."

"He's such a sweet little boy." Ms. Tobin smiled. "And so is Annie – a sweet little girl. So is my Miranda. Did you know that Annie told me at the adoption day the café held a while ago, that a little calico kitten was the right match for me? I called her Miranda after my childhood friend I lost contact with, but we found each other and now we exchange emails and phone calls all the time." She paused. "Well, I'm sure Mitch will solve the case. He's a good man, you know."

"I do," she replied. She'd only known him a short time, but she appreciated how he looked out for

Martha, particularly when she was in sleuthing mode, and Lauren seemed very happy in her marriage to him.

"What will you do for yoga now?" Ms. Tobin asked.

"I haven't thought about it yet. But I realized in class that it's been too long since I practiced regularly, so I'm hoping to find another class, or maybe try an online one."

"That is a good idea." Ms. Tobin nodded. "If you go online, there's no chance of anyone being murdered – I hope."

***

"This is downward dog, Teddy." Pru glanced at the TV screen that afternoon, copying the yoga instructor's moves.

"Ruff!" Teddy grinned at her sideways, putting Pru in mind of the way she and Zoe had chatted to each other during Sunny's yoga class as they practiced the pose.

"You're already doing it." She smiled back at him. She stood, getting into position for warrior one. "And this is—"

"Whatcha doing?" Martha entered the living room from the kitchen, eyeing Pru's work out gear. "Ooh – yoga. Lemme see."

Pru proceeded to demonstrate, following the online instructor's moves. "There are tons of videos online – and they're free," she explained.

"I think that's one of my favorite words – free." Martha's eyes lit up. "But I don't think I could do yoga." She sounded disappointed. "What about that pose you're always talking about – tree or bush or—"

"Tree pose." She stood on one leg, placing the other foot on the side of her leg between her ankle and her knee.

"How long can you stay like that?"

"A few minutes." She wobbled slightly, but regained her balance. "It's easier if you concentrate on staring at something."

"Like this?" Martha stuck her fingers in her ears and scrunched up her face, causing Pru to giggle and wobble again.

"Something boring," she replied, unable to hold her balance any longer, and planting her foot on the floor.

"Ruff!" Teddy agreed.

"Why don't you teach a class?" Martha suggested. "You seem to know a lot about it."

"Thanks, but I'm not certified."

"Oh, pooh. Who's going to know?"

"I will. And anyone who asks me what my qualifications are."

"Huh." Martha thought for a moment. 'You're probably right. What a shame. You'd be able to make some extra money as well. How much did you pay for that class?"

"Eighteen dollars."

"And there were how many girls there?"

"Eight, I think. But Sunny also had to pay rent on the space."

"Yeah – we gotta question Kevin, her landlord," Martha said. "I couldn't find out anything about this Sunny at the senior center today. No one seemed to have heard of her."

"That's a shame." Pru turned off the video.

"And how are we going to track down this Angela?"

"Hit every yoga studio in Sacramento?" She wondered how long that would take. Then she had an idea. "What would your retired lady detective in your script do?"

"Good one." Martha's face lit up. "She'd call the studios and ask for an Angela because her friend raved about her classes, and describe what she looks like."

"Ruff!" *Yes!*

"Then that's we'll do," Martha declared. "Gimme the phone book and I'll look up yoga classes."

"Do we have a telephone directory?" Pru glanced around the living room but couldn't remember seeing one.

"Oh, yeah." Martha pouted. "Now it's all online digital stuff. In the old days all I had to do was grab the directory, look up yoga, and it would all be laid out for me. Now I have to type in yoga on the computer and I guess Sacramento, and peer at the screen and—"

"Why don't I make a list?"

"Great idea." Martha grinned. "And I'll make us a hot chocolate."

Teddy looked up at her hopefully.

"And give my little guy a treat."

***

After the fifth call, Martha waved madly at her. "Yeah, that sounds like her," she told the person on the phone. Glancing up at Pru, she said, "Long black hair, right?"

"Yes."

"And what time does her class start?" Martha continued her phone conversation. "Eight o'clock tomorrow morning? Saturday? We've gotta book now? Put me down for two people then."

Pru stared at her friend. Was Martha really going to try yoga? Or was it just a ploy to snoop around while Pru took the class?

Martha ended the call, looked up, and grinned. "Better get your yoga outfit ready. We're going to Angela's class tomorrow morning!"

***

"Remind me why we're doing this," Martha grumbled the next morning. She wore turquoise sweatpants and matching sweater.

"Because you made the arrangements." Pru stifled a yawn and glanced at her roommate's outfit. "I hope you're not going to get too hot," she gently pointed out, driving down the quiet street.

"I didn't know what else to wear." Martha looked down at her clothes. "I'm not really a shorts and T-shirt kind of gal – not anymore, anyway."

"I understand."

"Teddy wanted to come, but he probably wouldn't be allowed in the studio, and I didn't want to leave him in the car," Martha said.

"I'm sure he'll be happier at home."

"Unless we uncover something in our sleuthing. Then he'll be upset he missed out on the action."

"I'm sure he'll get plenty more sleuthing action." After living with Martha and Teddy for the last six months, this seemed like a normal conversation to Pru now.

"What time is it, anyway?" Martha peered at Pru's wrist. "Not even seven a.m."

"We've got to find this studio," Pru replied, "and it does take at least an hour to drive to Sacramento."

"Maybe we can stop for a snack on the way home." Martha brightened. "A big, juicy burger and fries. And a shake, of course. Maybe chocolate."

"That sounds good." Her mouth watered, since she'd only had a tiny bowlful of fiber rich cereal for breakfast.

She drove along the highway, which thankfully wasn't too busy at that hour. Probably all the weekly commuters were at home still sleeping. A twinge of envy struck her, but she brushed it away. She'd get to attend another yoga class and she had to admit that the more she helped Martha with her sleuthing the more intriguing – and even addictive – it became.

Pru had looked up the address online. During the journey, Martha hummed out of tune, talked about the watercolor class at the senior center, and fiddled with the radio several times.

"Where are you up to in your retired lady detective script?" she asked.

"I'm still stuck," Martha admitted. "I've gotta come up with a way for her to solve the case and show up those two hotshot detectives who aren't so hot. Now she's played a prank on them, she needs to find who the killer is. And those two hotshots aren't sharing their information with her."

"That does sound tricky," Pru replied.

"Yeah. Maybe I should talk it over with Teddy and see what he suggests," Martha said in all seriousness.

"Good idea."

They reached Sacramento, and she managed to find her way to the yoga studio with only taking one wrong turn.

"Pretty good." Martha grinned and peered at Pru's watch. "And with five minutes to spare!"

Pru grabbed her yoga gear from the trunk, as well as the walker. She paused.

"Martha, you don't have a yoga mat."

"Oh yeah. I thought they could lend me one."

"Hopefully. Does this mean you're actually going to take the class as well?"

"Why not?" Martha shrugged. "It would look a bit suspicious if I snooped around outside while you did the actual yoga. Plus Angela is the instructor, so this way I should be able to get up close to her."

"If we get there in time." Pru tucked her rolled up mat under her arm.

"The competition is fierce in some sessions to be in the first row. If we're not there early enough, we'll be stuck in the back."

"Then we'd better get going!" Martha clutched the handles of her rolling walker and sped to the entrance of the modern dome-shaped building, made out of glass and steel. "Coming through!" she hollered, barreling in through the automatic doors. "Where's Angela's yoga class?" she asked the surprised eighteen-year-old at the reception desk.

"Names?" The girl's fingers were poised over the keyboard.

"Martha and Pru."

"Go down that hall and turn right. It's the first door."

"Thanks." Pru smiled at her, and hurried after Martha.

The door was closed but there was a small window at eye level. She peered in, not really surprised to see the space half full already.

"Come on." Pushing open the door, she gestured for Martha to follow.

"The front row's taken," Martha said in disappointment.

"But there are some spots in the second row," Pru pointed out.

Martha pushed her walker over to the second row, not seeming to notice the surprised looks by the other ladies, all of them clad in trendy yoga outfits.

"That's Angela," Pru whispered, subtly gesturing to the tall woman at the front of the class. Her raven hair hung down her back, and once again she wore black yoga pants and a white T-shirt.

"We've gotta catch her eye," Martha said. "Stand out from everyone else, so we get her attention."

"I don't think that will be a problem," Pru murmured, aware of Angela's gaze on them.

"Hello, ladies." Angela approached them. "I'm afraid I've never had a student who used a walker before.

But if you're comfortable sitting on the seat, I can show you how to do modified versions of some of the poses."

"That sounds good. I'm Martha, and this is Pru."

"Hi." Pru smiled, feeling a little as if she were undercover.

"Do I know you?" Angela's gaze sharpened. "Have we met recently?"

"I was at Sunny's yoga class in Gold Leaf Valley," she admitted.

"Yes. Now I recognize you." Angela nodded. "But what are you doing here if you like – liked – Sunny's style?"

"So you know she's dead?" Martha jumped in eagerly.

"I had heard. A detective interviewed me."

"That was probably Mitch," Martha told her.

"No, I'm sure he said his name was Jesse." Angela frowned. "He was tall, with dark wavy hair, and was quite good looking."

"Yeah, that was Jesse," Martha agreed. "He's Pru's beau."

"Martha," Pru hissed, nudging her.

"Well, someone's gotta get you two together."

Pru refrained from rolling her eyes and answered Angela's question instead.

"That was the first class I took with Sunny," she explained, "and I felt it wasn't the right style for me – before we discovered she had died."

"Yeah," Martha added sagely.

Pru was grateful her roommate didn't mention that *they* had been the ones to find Sunny's body.

"Where do I get one of these mats?" Martha pointed to Pru's, which was tucked under her arm.

"If you're not going to do floorwork, you won't need one," Angela replied.

"Oh." Martha sounded disappointed. "I guess that's right – if I get down on the floor, I might not be able to get up again!" she chuckled.

"Stay here in the second row," Angela told them, "and I'll keep an eye on you."

"Goody," Martha said cheerfully. Then she whispered in Pru's ear, "And I can keep an eye on her!"

CHAPTER 7

"Whatcha doing now?" Martha peered down at Pru from her seat on the walker.

"Cobra," Pru replied, keeping her eyes on Angela. She had to admit that Angela's style of teaching was one she was enjoying. Zoe might be interested in trying a class here.

"Like the snake?"

"Yes," she murmured.

"I bet my retired lady detective would like that one."

"Why don't you write it in the script?"

"Good idea." Martha nodded.

Martha sitting on her walking had been a focal point for the first part of the class, but as the session progressed, Pru was no longer aware of the other students' gazes upon them. She also noticed that Danielle did not seem to be in the room, nor Bridget. But why she expected or semi-expected her ex-best friend to be at this yoga class, she didn't know.

"Martha." Angela gestured to her. "Float your hands up toward your head, and then down again, like this." She made a floaty waving motion.

"I can do that!" Martha sounded enthused and waved her arms up and down like a semaphore signaler.

"Slower," Pru murmured beside her. "Don't wear yourself out."

"Right." Martha nodded and slowed her pace. "This is quite relaxing."

Angela told them to place their hands behind their back and interlace their fingers.

"That's a bit harder," Martha grumbled.

"Just do the best you can, everyone," Angela advised. "Go at your own pace."

When Angela announced it was time for tree pose, Martha called out, "Pru's good at that one!"

A few ladies chuckled, but Pru flushed and looked straight ahead.

"Sorry," Martha whispered a moment later. "Didn't mean to embarrass you."

"I know." She gave her friend a quick smile, then followed Angela's instructions, balancing on one leg and hoping she wouldn't wobble.

"I wish I could do that," Martha said wistfully, still sitting on her walker seat.

When it was time for relaxation in corpse pose, Martha looked around the room at everyone lying down with a blanket over them.

"Now I understand why you like doing this stuff," Martha said in a stage whisper. "It's not that bad."

"Thanks," Pru said wryly from her prone position on the floor.

When class was over and everyone broke into little groups to chat, Angela came over to them. "Did you enjoy the class, Martha?"

"It was a bit different to what I expected," Martha replied honestly. "It wasn't half bad."

"I enjoyed it," Pru said.

"I can see you've practiced for a while," Angela complimented her. "Keep it up."

"I hope to."

"I thought it was awful when Pru told me that Sunny stole your students," Martha said. "Had she worked for you long?"

"A few years," Angela replied. "Her style was not mine, but some people came here just to be in her class, and I couldn't afford to turn away anyone who paid."

"What about Danielle?" Pru remembered Sunny's fan. "I heard something about her becoming a teacher."

"Oh, Danielle." Angela looked amused and shook her head. "She's been talking about becoming a teacher for a while now, but as far as I know, she's never done anything about it. I think she could be a good teacher one day, when she has a little more maturity."

"Does she come to your class, too?" Martha looked around the room, but most of the ladies had departed now.

"She used to," Angela admitted. "And then she took Sunny's class one day and never returned to mine. Whenever I bumped into her here, she always raved about Sunny's style of teaching. I don't know what she'll do now that's Sunny's … gone."

"Can you think of anyone who might have had it in for Sunny?" Pru asked.

"Why?" Angela's gaze sharpened. "She fell down a flight of stairs."

"You mean the police didn't tell you that trip wire was involved?" Martha asked.

"What?"

"Martha!" Pru nudged her. "Maybe we shouldn't mention that."

"That nice detective Jesse didn't mention tripwire," Angela said. "What are you talking about?"

"We found the bod – Sunny," Martha admitted. "And saw a tripwire at the top of the stairs."

"Oh, no." Angela shuddered. "She could be difficult at times, and I was angry that she'd poached my students, but I don't know anyone who would be so incensed that they would kill her."

***

"I think I made a boo-boo," Martha mourned on the journey home. "I don't think I should have mentioned the trip-wire."

"No," Pru agreed, "I don't think you should have."

"I hope Mitch won't be cross if he finds out," Martha continued.

"Me too."

A while later, Martha ordered, "Stop here!" She pointed to a fast-food joint decorated in bright colors. "All that yoga has made me hungry."

Martha ordered a burger, fries, and chocolate shake for herself in the drive-thru. "What about you?"

"I'll have the same." Her tiny bowl of cereal seemed a long time ago. She peered at her watch, surprised to see it wasn't noon yet.

They munched on their burgers in the parking lot. Martha wadded up the napkins and wrappers and stuffed them into the paper bag. "I'll put this in the trash when we get home."

"Good idea." Pru started the ignition and rejoined the highway.

Soon, they reached the outskirts of Gold Leaf Valley.

"Is it okay if we stop at the café on the way home?" she asked. "Lauren said the other day she'd check with Father Mike about setting up a toy exchange for Teddy, Annie, and Mrs. Snuggle. She might have an update."

"Goody!" Martha's eyes lit up. "And we can get some cupcakes to go."

"After that big meal we just ate?" She'd slurped up her chocolate shake enthusiastically, and relished her burger and fries, but was now starting to regret it just a tad.

"We can have them for dessert tonight."

"That does sound nice."

Luckily, she was able to snag a parking spot right outside the café, a

Victorian building which adjoined a cottage Pru knew belonged to Lauren and Mitch.

"I can't wait to tell Annie about going undercover in the yoga class." Martha grabbed her walker once Pru got it out of the trunk.

"What about Lauren and Zoe?"

"Them, too." Martha chuckled. "Hopefully, they won't be too busy so we can all grab a table and have a good chat."

Martha's hopes became true. There were only a few customers inside, and Annie trotted to greet them. Pru could have sworn the silver-gray tabby's furry face lit up when she spied Martha.

"Jump up, cutie pie." Martha winked at the feline.

"Brrt!" Annie perched on the vinyl padded seat of the walker.

"Hi." Pru waved to Lauren and Zoe, who were both behind the counter.

"Ooh – did you do yoga this morning, Pru?" Zoe was dressed in a purple T-shirt and olive pants, and

zoomed out to intercept them.
"You've got the same outfit on you wore to Sunny's yoga class."

"I did, too," Martha replied proudly. "Well, I sat on my walker and did my best."

"Martha was able to do some poses," Pru added.

"Yeah, there was this floaty arm thing, where you move your arms up and down, up and down – oops!" In her enthusiastic demonstration, she accidentally bopped Zoe on her shoulder.

"Ow!" Zoe rubbed the sore spot.

"Sorry." Martha looked abashed.

"Why don't we sit down and tell you about it?" Pru suggested.

"Yeah, and give us an update on this toy exchange," Martha requested.

"Brrt!" Annie put in.

"First, do you want any cupcakes?" Zoe asked. "We've nearly sold out, so you'd better tell me now if you'd like any."

"You betcha!" Martha nodded vigorously. "Whatcha got?"

"Salted caramel, Norwegian apple, and super vanilla."

"We'd better have one of each," Martha decided. "Right, Pru?"

"I'm afraid so." Surely one and a half cupcakes today would be okay? She had just done seventy-five minutes of yoga, after all.

Zoe zipped back to the counter and returned in several seconds. "All set. And Lauren's able to take a break now and join us as well."

"Goody!"

"Brrt!" *Yes!*

Martha parked her walker at the rear table Annie had chosen for them, and sank down into the pine chair. Annie hopped from the walker to the seat next to Martha, and Pru sat opposite them. Zoe plonked down next to Pru, and placed the cupcake box in the middle of the table.

"Oops – I forgot to ask if you'd like a latte or cappuccino," Zoe said. "Or Martha's favorite – hot chocolate."

"That's tempting." Martha turned and looked longingly at the counter.

Lauren was just rounding the corner and walking to join them. "But we stopped for a snack on the way home. Besides, if Lauren's making the drinks, then she'll miss out on hearing our news."

"What news is that?" Lauren asked, sitting next to Annie. "Oh, Pru, I've got a toy exchange update for you. In fact—" her hazel eyes sparkled "—Father Mike brought a toy over to lend to Teddy, chosen by Mrs. Snuggle. And she lent Annie a toy yesterday, as well."

"That's great." Pru smiled.

"Yeah, it's a soft unicorn," Zoe said.

"Annie loves it," added Lauren. "Let me get Teddy's toy before I forget." She rose and hurried to the counter. When she returned she held out a small paper bag to Martha.

"Thanks!" Martha pulled out the pink ball and held it up. "Teddy is gonna have a lot of fun with this." She handed it to Pru.

"He'll love it," she agreed, just imagining the little white furball running after it in the yard. "And Mrs. Snuggle's already given him back the bear he lent her a while ago."

"How was yoga?" Zoe asked.

"I enjoyed it," Pru replied. "In fact, you might like trying Angela's class. She's a good teacher."

"We were undercover," Martha said proudly. "Until the end when I let out that there had been trip wire involved in Sunny's death."

"You what?" Lauren's eyes widened. "Oh, no."

"Brrt," Annie scolded Martha.

"I know." Martha grimaced. "I'm sorry. And I ended up telling Angela we found Sunny's body."

"Did you find out anything, though?" Zoe asked eagerly.

"Not much," Martha admitted.

"But it sounds like Danielle talks a lot about becoming a teacher but isn't doing much to get qualified," Pru said.

"Yeah, remember when Sunny asked her at the end of class if she'd enrolled in the teacher training course?" Zoe nodded. "And she said she was on the waitlist."

"What if there isn't a waitlist?" Martha suggested. "She could have made the whole thing up!"

"So Sunny wouldn't get mad at her," Pru put in thoughtfully.

"So the next thing we have to do is talk to this Danielle," Martha said. "I didn't see her at class this morning, did you?"

"No," Pru replied. "Angela did say she doesn't come to her class anymore once she discovered Sunny's style of teaching."

"So what is she going to do now?" Zoe asked. "Since Sunny's – you know."

"She'll have to find another instructor," Lauren put in.

"Hey!" Zoe snapped her fingers. "If I knew more about yoga, I could pose as an instructor and ..."

"Pru knows a lot about yoga," Martha declared.

She froze as they all looked at her, including Annie.

"But I'm not qualified to teach," she said quickly.

"Like I said before, who's going to know?" Martha winked.

"This could be the perfect plan," Zoe said enthusiastically. "You could hold a yoga class to try and lure Danielle—"

"Lure? I'm not luring anyone."

"You don't have to do anything you're not comfortable with doing, Pru," Lauren spoke. "Right, Zoe? Martha? Annie?"

There was a tiny silence.

"Brrt." *Right.*

"I guess you're right," Zoe conceded.

"Yeah," Martha grumbled. She looked across the table at Pru. "But you will think about it, won't you? Zoe's spot-on. It could be the perfect plan."

"I'll think about it," she conceded. "That's all."

***

"I really don't think this is a good idea," Pru said that evening, devouring half a Norwegian Apple cupcake. "Like I said, I'm not qualified to teach a yoga class. What if someone finds out and puts in a complaint?"

"To who?" Martha forked up a piece of salted caramel cupcake. "You don't belong to a yoga organization, do you?"

"No."

"Then who can they complain to?"

"The police?" she hazarded a guess.

"What if you put on the poster that you're not a real teacher?" Martha proposed. "You could say, you're a yoga enthusiast and you're teaching the class as a yoga enthusiast."

"I guess," Pru replied. "But …" Just the thought of standing in front of a group of people and showing them the different poses made her feel shy. How could she do that in reality? It was totally different being a student in a yoga class and following the teacher's instructions.

"I bet you could hold the class in the same place," Martha continued. "Where Sunny died."

"You mean where Sunny was murdered." She stared at her friend.

"Ruff!" Teddy agreed. He'd been hanging around the kitchen table hoping for scraps, but cupcakes were not a canine food. When they'd returned home from the café, he'd scolded them for being away for so long, and they'd apologized and spent plenty of time playing with him in the yard to make up for their morning trip without him.

"I could keep watch outside at the top of the stairs," Martha suggested. "So if anyone tries to kill you with trip wire, I can stop them."

Pru's eyes widened. "Why would anyone want to kill me?"

"See, I've been thinking this afternoon," Martha replied. "What if Sunny wasn't killed because she was Sunny? What if she was murdered because she was a yoga teacher? Maybe there's a yoga teacher serial killer running around. So if you teach the class, you might be next!"

"Then why would I teach a class?" Pru pointed out. "Unless you want someone to kill me?" She leaned back in her chair.

"Of course not, silly." Martha patted her hand. "I was just trying to think of all the possible angles. I think it's a great idea, you teaching a class. It might lure all sorts of people who had a problem with Sunny, and then we can question them!"

"Unless one of them kills me first," Pru tried to joke.

"I know! Let's ask Jesse to come. You never know, he might be into all that sort of stuff." Martha winked. "And if he's not, maybe we could hire him as your bodyguard."

"My body what?" She blushed at the thought of Jesse guarding her body.

"Your bodyguard," Martha repeated with a chuckle. "Isn't that what off duty police officers do? They do PI work and bodyguard stuff and—"

"How do you know that?" Pru asked.

"Oh, you know." Martha waved a hand in the air. "I pick up a lot of interesting tidbits from TV shows and movies."

"I'm sure Jesse wouldn't be interested in being my bodyguard," Pru said after a moment. "He's probably not interested in yoga, either. So I don't think we should bother hm about this yoga class."

"So you're going to teach it?" Martha asked eagerly. "Goody! I'll call Mitch right now and see if we can hire Sunny's studio."

"It could still be a crime scene." Pru crossed her fingers behind her back. She hoped so. What had she let Martha talk her into? She wasn't a yoga teacher – and if Martha had her way, the whole town would know it as well.

Teddy watched with interest as Martha pressed the buttons on her cell phone. "Mitch? It's me. Martha. Yes, I'm good, thanks for asking. Pru wants to teach a yoga class and we were thinking she could do it in Sunny's studio – you know, where Sunny was found at the bottom of the stairs and—"

Pru overheard Mitch's voice but couldn't quite make out the words. But from Martha's expression, it wasn't what she wanted to hear.

"Well, pooh." Martha pouted. "That's no good." She paused. "Yeah, I'm sorry for blabbing about the trip wire stuff." Then she heaved a sigh. "Fine. Ooh – tell Jesse about this, won'tcha? Maybe he's into yoga." A moment later, she ended the call.

"Mitch says it's still a crime scene."

"Oh. Well, if we can't do it, we can't do it, so …"

"I never give up so fast." Martha screwed up her face in thought. "I know!" She started pressing buttons on her phone again. "I bet Father Mike would let us use the church hall. Yeah! And I can thank him for lending Teddy Mrs. Snuggle's ball as well."

Pru's heart sank while Martha made the call. Teddy jumped up on his hind legs and put his head on her knees.

"You know you're not supposed to do that," she whispered, stroking his soft, cottony fur, "but I won't tell if you don't."

"Wuff," Teddy mumbled softly, laying the side of his head on her knee.

"I don't really want to teach this class," she confessed to him, keeping her voice low while Martha spoke to Father Mike. "But if it helps the case, maybe I should get out of my comfort zone and do it."

"Wuff," Teddy seemed to agree.

"Father Mike said yes!" Martha grinned, ending the call. "He said you can have your pick of late afternoon or evenings next week. And he's only going to charge a ten-dollar fee for the hall."

"That's very reasonable," Pru replied. It looked like she would have to get out of her comfort zone and stand in front of everyone and teach yoga. Then another thought struck her. What if no one came? She didn't know if that would be even worse.

"He didn't want to charge us anything at first," Martha continued, oblivious to Pru's inner turmoil, "but I insisted we pay him ten dollars. I mean, you're gonna make something, right? How much did you pay for Sunny's class? Today Angela charged us twenty dollars each!

"Ooh, I know," Martha added. "We can hold it on Tuesday, and then I bet that everyone who came to Sunny's class will come to yours."

"Ruff!" Teddy had jumped down and now trotted over to Martha's chair.

"See? Teddy thinks it's a good idea." Martha beamed, stroking the little white dog.

"Well, if Teddy thinks so …" she smiled at the Coton, telling herself this whole experience would be good for her.

"I'll make the posters," Martha declared. "And you can put one up at the library, and Lauren and Zoe will have one up at the café, and—"

"But how are we going to make sure Danielle sees one of your posters?" Pru asked. "We don't even know where she lives or hangs out."

"That's a toughie." Martha nodded. "I guess we can't whizz back to Sacramento and stick up a poster at Angela's studio?"

"No, we can't," Pru replied firmly.

"Huh." Martha screwed up her face in thought. "Well, I guess if she doesn't turn up, we'll just have to ask Mitch where we can find her."

"Do you think he'll tell you?" Pru looked at her doubtfully.

"If he doesn't, someone must know something about her. I know!" Martha's expression lifted. "Maybe one of those other ladies at Sunny's class will come to yours, and then we can ask her about Danielle. We could say we don't want her to miss out on a new yoga experience."

"It will definitely be a new experience," Pru said with feeling.

CHAPTER 8

Martha created the posters on Sunday the old-fashioned way – with white paper and a black marker.

"Who's that?" Pru tapped a stick figure in the middle.

"That's you." Martha grinned. "I'm not too good at drawing, apart from my watercolor class – sort of – so that's my third attempt. I thought it would be fun if they saw what you looked like – but your hair is auburn and I don't have a red marker, so I had to make do."

"Did you say I'm not a qualified teacher?" She didn't want to mislead anyone.

"Yep. Down here." Martha pointed to the bottom of the poster, where in smaller block letters it said, "Taught by Pru, a real yoga enthusiast!"

She scanned the rest of the poster. The time, date, and location were all correct, assuming everyone in town knew exactly where 'Father Mike's church hall' was.

"You haven't mentioned how much I'm charging," she pointed out.

"Good one." Martha pulled the cap off the marker and looked at her expectantly. "Well?"

"Twelve dollars?"

"Is that all?" Martha tsked. "Angela had tons of ladies in her class yesterday – just imagine how much she made!"

"I thought we were doing this for sleuthing purposes, not profit purposes," Pru said. "I'll donate all the money to the church – if anyone comes."

"Don't worry." Martha reassured her. "Let's make a list of people you know who were in Sunny's class with you."

"Doris," Pru started, "Zoe—"

"Ooh, I bet Zoe will come," Martha broke in eagerly. "She might drag Lauren along, too. And if you ask Doris real nice, I bet she'd attend."

"She might," Pru conceded. Then she had a thought. "But I don't like the idea of charging my friends."

"Maybe you could give them a special rate for pals." Martha winked.

"But then it wouldn't be fair to the other students – if there are any."

"Huh." Martha tapped the marker on the table. "Yeah, I can see how you might feel about that, because you're very ethical. And I promised Father Mike ten dollars to use the church hall. So just tell me a figure you're comfy with."

Pru eventually decided on an even lower figure of eight dollars.

"Okay." Martha nodded. "That's very reasonable. Ooh – I can put up a poster tomorrow at the senior center. And I bet Brooke would be interested. And Claire. She always looks so athletic."

"She does," Pru replied. Claire was tall, blonde, and slim, and wore yoga pants. If her husband was home from work he could look after their young daughter Molly, or Molly could attend as well. But would it be safe for a little girl to be there if the purpose of this class was to lure potential suspects?

"How is this going to attract everyone at Sunny's class? There were only three locals – me, Zoe, and Doris. The rest seemed to be ladies from Sacramento and—"

"Bridget." Martha made a face. "Hopefully she won't find out about it. I don't see how she could be the killer, anyway. She's just blown into town and once she sees she can't worm her way into your good books, she'll blow back out again."

"Do you think so?" Pru had been trying not to think about her ex-best friend at all – with mixed results.

"Trust me." Martha nodded sagely. "I've met all sorts in my time. It might not seem like it now, but she did you a favor by using you to cheat on her exams. Because otherwise, how would we have met?"

"Ruff!"

***

Monday night, Pru studied up on yoga poses. She didn't want to do the exact same routine as Sunny or Angela, but she needed the postures to flow into each other and also make sense. And she had to be mindful that there might only be beginners in the class, and some of them may never have tried yoga before. Like Lauren.

By the time she turned off her bedside light, it was almost midnight. She finally drifted off to sleep fretting that nobody would turn up, and their sleuthing plan would be a flop.

***

The next morning, Pru gulped down her fiber rich but flavorless cereal when Martha's phone rang.

"You are?" Martha's face lit up and she waved wildly to Pru, although she sat across from her at the table. "Goody. I'll tell her." She banged the phone down on the table, next to her raisin toast, the scent tempting Pru to try it one day instead of her cereal.

"Lauren and Zoe are coming tonight. I called them yesterday about it. So that's two people already. And a few people read my poster at the senior center yesterday, so maybe at least one of them will attend."

"Doris popped into the library yesterday and I asked her to give it a try," Pru said.

"So that's four already." Martha grinned. "This is easy. Maybe you should do this regularly, like a side whatsie."

"Side hustle?"

"Yeah!" Martha pointed a finger at her.

"Ruff!" Teddy agreed, after dropping Mrs. Snuggle's pink ball from his mouth.

"Maybe," she replied, thinking *Probably not.*

The rest of the morning passed quickly – too quickly. Yesterday, she'd pinned up one of Martha's posters on the community board, after first getting Barbara's approval. Her boss had looked at her a little oddly – perhaps she'd never thought of Pru doing yoga, let alone trying to teach a class – but gave her permission.

"As long as it doesn't intrude on your work time," Barbara said.

"No, it won't," Pru promised.

Now, she could glance at the poster from her position at the returns desk. Every time she saw the stick figure of herself, it made her smile. Martha was a good friend. So was Teddy. Martha was right – Bridget *had* done her a favor by using her to cheat in college, even though it had felt like the worst thing in the world at the time. Even though she'd lived in Gold Leaf Valley for less than a year, she couldn't imagine *not* living here. Of course, she missed her family in Colorado, but even if the cheating scandal hadn't happened, she might have ended up accepting a job in another state, anyway.

After her lunchbreak, she started unpacking a box of books that had arrived earlier. When she saw the book Ms. Tobin had reserved, she called her right away with the good news.

"Wonderful!" Ms. Tobin said on the other end of the line. "I'll be there this afternoon."

Pru smiled as she put down the receiver. At least one patron would be satisfied today. This morning, Barbara had helped a woman at the reference desk, but apparently her search for the best way to make pancakes in the nineteenth century using a wood fueled stove hadn't met that patron's expectations, and she'd left the library muttering to herself.

Pru had just finished processing all the books in the box when Ms. Tobin arrived, slightly out of breath, wearing a taupe skirt and cream blouse.

"Thank you, Pru." Ms. Tobin allowed her to check out the book for her, then eagerly looked at the mystery cover. "I can't wait to start reading it when I get home."

"You're welcome," she replied. "I hope you'll enjoy it."

"I'm sure I will." Ms. Tobin smiled. She turned to leave, then swiveled on her heel. "I meant to ask you, what's this about you teaching a yoga class? I heard about it at the senior center today – not that I go often – and I didn't think that could be right."

"It is," Pru replied, gesturing to the poster on the board. "It's tonight, if you're interested." She hoped her voice hadn't squeaked a bit at the end.

"Maybe if I was younger," Ms. Tobin said, then shook her head. "No, I don't think yoga is for me. I'm sorry, I didn't realize how advanced you must be if you're teaching a class. I hope it goes well."

"Me too," she replied.

Ms. Tobin waved goodbye, the novel tucked under her arm.

She started shelving books, Ms. Tobin's words uppermost in her mind. Was she really advanced enough to teach yoga? What if someone got injured? What if there was someone in the class better than her and left halfway through because she – or he – thought Pru was doing it all wrong? By the time she arrived home that afternoon, she was ready to call the whole thing off.

"There you are." Martha grinned at her when she walked into the duplex.

"Ruff!" Teddy trotted to greet her.

She bent down to stroke him.

"I bumped into Brooke today at the café between her hair appointments and told her about tonight, and she said she'll definitely come. She's been wanting to try yoga for a while."

"Oh," she said faintly.

"So you should be making a profit already, even if you pay Father Mike the ten-dollar fee."

"I think I mentioned I'm going to give all the money to Father Mike."

"That's because you're a good girl." Martha nodded in approval. "What time does it begin?" She peered at Pru's watch.

"In just over an hour."

"Do you want dinner first or after?"

"After." She didn't think she could eat a thing right now, despite barely touching her lunch. "Martha, I don't think—"

"Just imagine if we get tons of suspects there tonight." Martha looked like she wanted to rub her hands in glee.

"We?"

"Didn't I tell you? I'm coming, too. We need both of us to question any suspicious characters."

"Ruff!" Teddy agreed.

"Is Teddy coming or staying home?"

"Wuff?" Teddy looked up hopefully at Martha.

"I wanna take you, little guy," Martha said slowly, "but I don't want you getting too excited at all the people doing funny movements."

"They'll be slow movements," Pru put in.

"Well …" Martha hesitated. "If it's okay with you, Pru, then I would like to bring him."

"Ruff!" *Goody!*

"But you have to be on your best behavior," Martha said.

"He usually is," Pru said.

"That's true." Martha nodded. "And he *is* a member of the senior sleuthing club, so he shouldn't miss out on a sleuthing experience."

"Ruff!"

"Maybe Teddy will want to do the yoga moves," Pru said, thinking back to the little dog joining her in the living room the other day when she was practicing.

"That would be a hoot." Martha chuckled.

She realized that now there was no way of backing out of taking the class. With a sigh, she changed into her outfit of yoga pants and blue T-shirt.

"Are you ready?" she asked Martha a short while later.

"We're going now?" Martha looked up from the sofa, closing her magazine in surprise.

Teddy jumped off the sofa and ran to Pru.

"I see my little guy is raring to go." Martha trundled toward them with her walker, wearing fuchsia sweatpants and matching top.

"I need to open up the hall and take the money," she replied. "And welcome everyone."

"Yeah, I guess if someone comes super early and you're not there, they might think the whole thing is cancelled. And if they're a suspect – or even the killer – that would be a disaster!"

Pru grimaced as she led them to her silver SUV parked right outside.

During the short drive to the church hall, Pru tried to center herself, her stomach a bundle of nerves. Just as well she hadn't eaten any dinner. When she reached the hall, she was relieved to see there weren't any other cars in the parking lot.

"What are you going to do while I'm teaching the class?" She turned to Martha.

"Me and Teddy will supervise," Martha declared. "And sniff out any people who look like suspects."

"How are you going to do that?"

"You'll find out." Martha tapped her nose.

She just hoped it didn't involve Martha interrupting her class to question a likely 'suspect'.

Pru found the spare key hidden above the lintel and unlocked the door. Wooden floorboards squeaked under her feet in the bare and empty space. Perfect for a yoga or exercise class.

"I brought a notebook." She pulled it out of her bag. "So I can write down everyone who attends and if they pay."

"*When* they pay," Martha said confidently. "Don't start the class until they pay you first."

"Good idea." She nodded.

Martha trundled around the room while Pru laid out her yoga mat, helped by Teddy.

"Wuff?" He sat on the mat and looked at her expectantly.

She laughed.

"You can be my helper, Teddy." She stroked him along his shoulder.

"Ruff!" His brown eyes sparkled.

"Hi!" Zoe zoomed into the hall, followed by Lauren.

"Hi." She smiled in relief. At least there were two people here, and more importantly, they were her friends.

"Oh, goody." Martha waved at them from the other side of the room.

"Are you going to do yoga too, Martha?" Lauren asked.

"No." Martha chuckled. "Well, I might do the floaty arm thing again if Pru does that one, but me and Teddy are going to sniff out suspects while Pru does her thing."

"Good thinking." Zoe nodded. Rolling out her mat, she said to Pru, "We're going to be in the front row."

"So you have friendly faces," Lauren added.

"Thanks." Pru smiled at them.

"I made Lauren buy a mat," Zoe put in.

"I haven't tried this before," Lauren said. "I hope that's okay."

"Of course it is," Pru assured her. "Don't worry, last week was Doris's first class as well. We'll be doing gentle poses."

"That's a relief," Zoe said, "especially after the torture Sunny put us through. I wonder if that girl Danielle is going to turn up?"

"I hope not," Pru replied, although Martha would probably be disappointed if she didn't attend.

Doris arrived next with a shy smile, and then looked down at her jeans. "I didn't have time to buy yoga pants," she apologized.

"You're welcome wearing anything you like," Pru told her. "As long as you're comfortable in it."

"I am," Doris assured her. She took her place next to Zoe and unrolled her mat.

"Hi, guys!" Brooke, the local hair stylist, rushed in. Her chestnut locks had attractive reddish highlights, cut in a long bob with feathered ends. The hair color flattered her friendly green eyes. She wore black yoga pants and an emerald T-shirt.

"Hi!" Claire appeared, wearing her usual outfit of yoga pants and a T-shirt.

"Where's Molly?" Zoe looked around the room as if expecting to see the little blonde girl suddenly appear.

"At home with my husband." Claire laughed. "She wanted to come, but I told her tonight it's Mommy time. She's playing with her cat Kitty right now."

Two ladies trickled in, who Pru thought might have been in Sunny's class. Everyone made a fuss of Teddy, and Pru realized this was the perfect moment to ask for payment.

"Teddy would like to check you off in his book." She placed the notebook in front of the Coton. "It's eight dollars each."

"Here, Teddy." Zoe put the cash on the mat next to his front paws. He looked up at her with a smile, and placed his paw over the bills.

Everyone laughed in delight and lined up for Teddy to take their money. Pru had just marked off everyone on her list, when a new voice said, "I hope you're not starting without me!"

CHAPTER 9

Pru's stomach lurched. It was Bridget. She stared at her ex-best friend. What on earth was she doing here?

"I saw the poster at the café today," Bridget said, her caramel hair glossy and shiny. She wore the outfit she'd worn at Sunny's class – gold yoga pants and a black top criss-crossing over her back.

"Drat," Martha grumbled under her breath.

"It will be fun to take a class with you," Bridget continued. "I didn't know you taught."

"I guess you do now," was all Pru could come up with.

"Ruff!" Teddy looked at Bridget, then down at the notebook next to his paws.

"Teddy is asking you to pay," Zoe told her. "It's eight dollars."

"Oh. Right." Bridget dug in her purse and gave Teddy some crumpled bills.

Teddy quickly placed his paw over the money.

"Thanks," Pru said. "We might as well get started." To her relief, the first row was full, which meant that Bridget had to take her place in the second.

She tried to tell herself not to think about Bridget, but couldn't help wondering if her ex-friend would criticize her choice of postures.

Pru started them off with floating arms, which Martha joined in with relish, sitting on her walker. Then she took them through warrior one, two, and three, constantly reminding everyone to go at their own pace.

Soon, she was caught up in the flow of the movements, trying to watch everyone at once in case she needed to correct their stance. With a start, she realized she was enjoying herself. Maybe she was a little more advanced than she thought?

Toward the end of the class, when everyone apart from Martha was in downward dog, the door flew open.

Her eyes widened. Jesse stood in the doorway, wearing black shorts and a white T-shirt.

"What are you doing here?" she blurted, hoping she wasn't going to blush.

"Who's that?" she heard Bridget murmur appreciatively.

Half the class abruptly ended the pose to look at Jesse, while the other half held it.

"I thought you might be into this sort of stuff," Martha said gleefully.

"Sorry, I'm late," Jesse said. "I got held up."

"Did Mitch tell you Jesse does yoga?" she heard Zoe stage whisper to Lauren.

"No." Lauren shook her head.

"We've almost finished." Pru cleared her throat. "But there's room in the second row."

"You mean the back," Jesse said good naturedly.

Unfortunately, he took the spot next to Bridget.

Once Pru encouraged everyone to try downward dog again, she couldn't help wondering what Jesse was doing here. She hadn't expected him to come, and now that he had, she wasn't sure if she liked it or not. When she led them into a crescent lunge, she peeked at him through the gap in the first row. Bridget was saying something to him, but Jesse seemed to be focused on his pose more than replying to her.

After their five-minute relaxation, Pru ended the class.

"Thank you for coming, everyone," she called out.

"I'm glad I tried it again," Doris said.

"That was fun!" Zoe grinned.

"Yes, it was." Lauren sounded a little surprised. "You're a good teacher, Pru."

"Thanks." She smiled.

"Ruff!" Teddy agreed.

One of the ladies she didn't know came up to her. "Danielle asked me to check out your class and report back to her. She wanted to come tonight but she's trying a new hot yoga class in Sacramento."

"How did you find out about this evening?" Pru asked.

"Her grandmother is friends with a lady who lives here, and she saw the poster about it at the senior center. So she called Danielle's grandmother to tell her because she thought Danielle might be interested, especially now that Sunny is … gone."

"Did you know Sunny?" Martha suddenly pounced. Pru hadn't realized she'd been nearby.

"I only took her class a few times as her schedule didn't work for me, but Danielle raved about her. She's very upset about Sunny's death." Her accusing tone made it sound like it was all Pru's fault. "I can't believe you didn't do boat pose," the woman continued. "Why not?"

"Because it's advanced," she replied, "and some of the class are beginners. I don't want anyone to strain themselves."

"You didn't do camel pose, either." The woman shook her head in annoyance. "Just wait until I tell Danielle."

"You do that," Martha retorted. "You were lucky to be in Pru's class tonight."

"Humph!" The woman stalked off, and the other woman they didn't recognize scurried after her.

"How about grabbing a coffee?" she heard Bridget asking Jesse. "We can discuss yoga and … other things." The way she was making eyes at Jesse, it was pretty obvious to Pru what 'other things' might mean.

"Thanks, but I can't make it tonight," Jesse replied, rolling up his black mat.

"Well, I'll still be in town later this week if you change your mind," Bridget persisted. "I'm staying at the local motel."

"Fortunately it's a nice place and not a no tell motel." Zoe giggled to Pru.

"It is." After all, she'd stayed there when she'd first moved to Gold Leaf Valley.

"I'm very busy with work," Jesse replied.

"Oh – too bad." Bridget looked at him regretfully.

Pru couldn't help feeling a little gleeful at the way Jesse had turned down Bridget's advances. Once again, she wondered how she'd ever been friends with her.

"Hey, Pru, are you holding another class?" Bridget sauntered over to her.

"I'm not sure," she replied cautiously.

"Let me know if you do. Oh, did you talk to your boss about a job for me?"

"No." She stared at Bridget. And frowned.

"It would be great if you did." Bridget smiled in a slightly wheedling way.

"No, it wouldn't." Martha came to stand next to her.

"Ruff!"

"They're right." Pru straightened her shoulders. "You need to find your own job. And I told you, the library isn't hiring, anyway."

"Is there a problem, ladies?" Jesse approached.

"The only problem is you're not having coffee with me tonight." Bridget winked at him, then slowly looked from Jesse to Pru and back again, her expression dawning. "Jesse wasn't your dinner date after Sunny's class last week was he, Pru?"

She blinked, then remembered what Zoe had said about Pru meeting someone for dinner, which had been Martha and Teddy.

"Well, good for you," Bridget said in a slightly patronizing way. "Goodbye – for now."

There was a short silence after the door banged shut after Bridget.

"Thanks for coming, everyone," Pru tried to sound as if that conversation – or was it confrontation? – didn't happen.

"Let me know if you hold another class," Brooke said. "I really enjoyed it."

"Me too." Claire nodded. "Wait until I tell Molly about it – she's going to be upset she missed visiting with Teddy, though."

"Maybe she can come next week," Martha said.

Pru looked at her in surprise.

"Me and Pru have gotta talk about it first," Martha added hastily.

She heard a little snort of laughter and looked suspiciously at Jesse, who returned her glance with a bland expression.

"Ruff!" Teddy patted the notebook next to his paw. He'd sat next to Pru's mat the whole time during the session.

Zoe giggled. "Teddy wants you to pay up, Jesse. It's eight dollars."

"Sure." He dug in his shorts for his wallet.

"You don't have to pay the full amount," Pru told him hastily. "You weren't here the whole time."

"I should," he insisted, placing the money in front of Teddy.

"Pru's donating all the money from tonight to Father Mike and the church," Martha put in.

"He's a good man." Jesse smiled.

Everyone murmured agreement before filing their way out of the hall. Pru turned off the lights and locked up.

"Did the senior sleuthing club make any progress tonight?" Jesse's voice held a hint of laughter as he stood next to her.

"Nope," Martha answered glumly for Pru. "Only two possible suspects, and I didn't get a chance to question them."

CHAPTER 10

As Pru drove home, she realized Jesse hadn't answered her earlier question as to why he'd turned up at her class. Was he really into yoga? Or had Mitch asked him to keep an eye on the senior sleuthing club?

Thinking back to the way he'd moved during class, she could tell that he'd practiced yoga before.

"You're a good teacher," Martha praised. "I tried to do as much as I could sitting down."

"I noticed."

"Floaty arms is my favorite, though," Martha continued.

"Ruff!"

They both laughed, Pru remembering how Teddy's eyes had widened when he watched everyone moving their arms above their head and back down again.

"You're good at that tree pose," Martha said. "Better than Bridget.

She was awfully wobbly on each leg."

"She was?" She'd been so busy maintaining her own balance as well as checking everyone in the front row that she hadn't had a chance to look at the back row participants. Did that make her a bad teacher?

"We've got one lead, though," Martha told her. "That woman said Danielle's grandma is a friend of someone at the senior center. So all I have to do tomorrow is go and discover who that is."

"Do you think you'll be successful?" How many people would Martha need to talk to in order to find out?

"I may not have found out much tonight, but you wait – it'll be Danielle's grandma's friend – or bust!"

***

The next day, Pru couldn't help humming under her breath as she marked off the returned books at the library.

She was so glad she hadn't backed out of teaching the class last night. Maybe Martha was right and she should hold it again next week? Would Jesse be there? Her mind drifted to the way he'd looked in his shorts and T-shirt, his muscles delineated through the cotton fabric. She didn't blame Bridget for appreciating his form, but that didn't mean she wanted her to invite him for coffee. He'd turned her down, anyway. She didn't want to think about how she'd feel if he had gone for coffee with Bridget.

"You didn't do boat pose."

Pru sucked in a surprised breath at the accusation. Jerking her head up from the scanner, her eyes widened when she saw Danielle standing in front of the desk.

"That's right, I didn't. If you're talking about last night." She tried to keep her voice even.

"My friend told me." Danielle nodded, her tight ash-blonde ponytail bouncing. She wore form-fitting blue jeans and a delicate lace top. "And you didn't do camel pose, either. What kind of yoga instructor are you?"

"One who's mindful of people's limitations," Pru replied, glancing toward the reference desk. Barbara was busy with a patron's request, but she didn't want to attract her boss's attention. She was still mindful of the way Barbara had seemed annoyed when Bridget had come into the library asking her to help her get a job.

"Just wait until I get qualified as a teacher," Danielle continued. "Everyone will come to my classes instead of yours."

"When will you get qualified?" Pru said. "You know, you can teach if you're not."

"Like you?" Danielle frowned. "If I'm going to teach, I want to do it right. I'm going to make my mark in the yoga world, just like Sunny did. In fact, I'll dedicate my classes to Sunny's style of teaching and I'll get tons of students." She sighed. "It's just too bad that Sunny won't be here to see it. I miss her so much."

"I'm sorry," Pru sympathized. She didn't think she and Danielle would ever be friends, but she could hear the pain in her voice.

Suddenly aware of being watched, Pru turned her head, her gaze meeting with Barbara's. Her boss still sat at the reference desk but stared directly at Pru. "Is there anything library related I can help you with?" she asked.

"In this tiny place?" Danielle scoffed. "Nope. I just came to let you know your yoga class was lame."

"O-kay." Pru picked up the scanner and aimed it at the barcode of the next returned book.

"Is that all you're going to say?" Danielle's tone sounded huffy.

"Yes." Pru picked up the next book and scanned it. "I'm at work. I have work to do. And my boss is aware of your presence."

"She is?" Danielle sounded surprised and looked around wildly. "Where?"

"Over there." She tilted her head slightly toward the reference desk.

Danielle's eyes widened, then she turned and strode out of the library.

Pru let out a breath of relief a moment later. Why had Danielle even bothered to visit her? Just to tell her she didn't like the sound of her yoga class? Or maybe she was upset in some way because Pru had taught a class despite being unqualified, and that was something Danielle hadn't achieved yet?

Resolving to put it out of her mind, she concentrated on scanning all the returned books and placing them on a trolley.

A short while later, a tall man with dark hair walked in, wearing jeans and a blue-checked shirt. He looked around, as if not quite knowing where to go.

"May I help you?" Pru asked, thinking he looked familiar.

"Yes." He seemed relieved. "I've got this overdue fine but I swear I returned that book. There's no way I'm paying five bucks for something I didn't do."

"I understand." Recognition dawned when she heard his voice. "You're the landlord for Sunny's yoga studio, aren't you?"

He grimaced. "Don't mention her to me. She still owes me rent."

"She's dead." Pru couldn't avoid the shocked tone in her voice.

"I know. I sound like a horrible person, don't I?" He screwed up his face.

"Yes."

"Sunny and I had history. I did her a favor by renting out that upstairs space to her, after I spent some time sprucing it up, even though she couldn't pay me all the rent upfront. But I thought I'd give her a break. Even though …" he hesitated.

"Even though?" She held her breath.

"We used to date, but then she dumped me for a rich jerk. I wasn't successful enough for her. Then I found out later that he'd dumped her because she was too – too – drill-sergeantish."

"How did you find out that he dumped her?" Was she asking the right questions? After all, he was a suspect in Sunny's death – according to Martha, anyway.

"A friend of a friend told me," he replied, looking down at the returns desk. "Sunny didn't mention it when she called me out of the blue and asked if I had anything available that would be suitable for yoga classes."

"I see."

"But then she screwed me over like she always did." He shook his head. "By not paying all the rent. And now she's dead, she's not going to pay, is she? We didn't even have a proper lease – it was all verbal. Another favor I did her. I should have known better." He sounded disgusted at himself.

"I'm sorry." Pru didn't know what else to say.

"People think I must have money because I own a few properties, but after all the expenses I'm not left with all that much. And now I have an empty upstairs studio I need to rent, once the police have finished with it." He peered at her. "You were in Sunny's class, weren't you?"

"Yes."

"Why don't you and your pals get together and rent it from me? You can do your yoga and whatever other exercises you do in there. Make it a girls' night out."

She didn't know whether to giggle or not at his idea of a girls' night out. She thought Martha would hoot with laughter.

"Thanks, but last night I taught a yoga class at the church hall."

"Huh." He sized her up for a second. "There's more to you than meets the eye. Stealing Sunny's students already. She'd probably approve of that."

Barbara walked over to them. "Is there a problem, Pru?"

"Yeah, there's a problem," Kevin stated. "I'm not paying this bogus overdue fine." He waved the letter in the air. "I was just telling Pru here that I returned that book."

"I'm sure Pru can deal with it for you." Barbara gave her a look that said, *Deal with it efficiently and don't bother me about it.*

"I will, Barbara," Pru murmured.

"Good." Barbara returned to the reference desk.

"What was the name of the book?" she asked Kevin.

After he told her the title and author, she typed it into the computer. There was only one copy in the system.

"It should be on the shelf if it was returned." She strode to the Fs, aware of him following her, and quickly found it. "Here it is. I'm sorry. Sometimes the scanner misses the barcode and the return doesn't register in the system. I'll take care of your overdue fee." She held out her hand for the letter.

"Thanks," he replied gruffly. "You're okay."

Pru had just started returning books to the shelves after Kevin left, when a familiar voice made her heart sink.

"Hi, Pru."

Bridget.

"What are you doing here?" She'd said those same words last night to Jesse at yoga class.

"Looking for you," Bridget replied, wearing a pale pink shift dress that flattered her. "And your boss – Barb, is it?"

"Barbara," she replied through gritted teeth. "Why?"

"I'm going to ask her for a job, since you won't." Bridget frowned. "I don't know why you're not helping me. We'd have so much fun working together here. Hey! We could even be roomies, since there aren't many apartments around."

"I already have a roomie. Two, in fact." Just thinking of Martha and Teddy lifted her spirits.

"You mean the old lady at yoga last night?" Bridget scoffed. "You can't have fun with her with the way you can with me. We can go manhunting in Sacramento, for a start. You can't do that with her."

"Martha is my friend," Pru replied. "And I don't care to go manhunting."

"Oh, yeah, right, you've got that hunk Jesse. Lucky you." Bridget gave her an appraising look. "That's another reason why I should work here. It must be raining men. I don't remember you dating much in college."

"That's because I focused on my studies." And she hadn't met many guys that she'd really liked.

"Touche." Bridget laughed. "Okay, so where's your boss? I'll ask her right now."

"You can't—" But Bridget strode toward the reference desk. The patron Barbara was helping had just left.

After a second of staring after Bridget in shock, Pru raced to intercept her. "You can't ask—"

But it was too late. Bridget was already leaning over the reference desk, her wavy caramel hair dangling over her shoulders.

"Hi Barbara, I'm Bridget. We've met before. I'm Pru's best friend from college. I would just love to work here with Pru. She said you're the best boss she's ever had. I just love this little town – it's so quaint. I'm sure I could attract a younger demographic for you and really put this library on the map. What do you say?"

Pru was sure the expression on her face was of a startled deer. "I'm sorry, Barbara. I couldn't stop—"

"That's quite all right, Pru," Barbara said in a regal tone that she hadn't heard before. "I'll deal with this … matter." She looked Bridget up and down. "Only *real* librarians work in this library. What are *your* qualifications?"

"I studied at the same college as Pru," Bridget replied eagerly.

"Did you graduate?"

"Well, you see—"

"That's a no, then," Barbara said briskly. "I'm sure Pru has already told you we're not hiring at the moment."

"Yeah, you're not hiring other people, but surely you could make an exception for *me*?"

Pru wasn't sure if Barbara was going to burst into laughter or shout at Bridget to get out and never return.

"That is the funniest joke I've ever heard," Barbara said. But her tone did not sound amused. "Run off now, and graduate from college. Don't call me, because I'll never call you."

Pru's mouth parted. She admired Barbara for telling Bridget the facts so succinctly.

After a moment of stunned silence, Bridget protested, "But I want to work here."

"Too bad. I've already made my decision. You'll soon find out you can't always get what you want in life – what was your name again? – Bridget. Now please leave, so the real librarians in here can get their work done." Barbara turned her steely gaze to Pru. "I want all those returns shelved by lunch, Pru, and in the afternoon you'll be setting up the room for French conversation."

"Yes, Barbara." She hurried to the desk, not wanting to incur her boss's anger. But she couldn't help a slight smile. She mightn't be able to make Bridget hear her, but Barbara had. Maybe now Bridget would leave her alone – and even better – leave town.

"I can't believe she can't see how good I would be for this place," Bridget muttered, stalking toward the returns desk. "It's not fair, Pru. How did you get your job?"

"By winning it fairly and squarely," she couldn't resist saying. Picking up the scanner, she added, "I have to work now."

"But …" Bridget hesitated, then seemed to realize Pru was focused on her task. "Okay." She heaved a sigh, then headed toward the exit.

Once Bridget left, Barbara strode over to her.

"I'm sorry, Barbara," she said. "I told her the library wasn't hiring but Bridget wouldn't listen to me."

"Don't worry about her, Pru," Barbara replied briskly. "I've met her type before. But I don't want to see her in here again."

"No," she agreed, wondering how she could possibly stop Bridget from entering the library unless she was right there at the door, shelving tomes in that particular bookcase.

Barbara strode back to the reference desk, her gaze fastening onto the computer screen.

As she placed books back on the shelves, Pru thought she'd had a lucky escape from Barbara's wrath. She shook her head at Bridget's presumption, but really, was that anything new? Once again she realized she hadn't learned much about her friend in college until Bridget had used her to cheat.

She couldn't wait to sink down on the sofa and talk about her day with Martha and Teddy. Afterward, she could take Teddy for a walk, or play in the yard with him. And maybe she could persuade Martha that they should have an emergency pizza night.

"Ruff!" The sound of thundering paws greeted her as she opened the front door that afternoon. Teddy was a small dog but he had large, fluffy white paws.

"Hi." Pru bent down to tickle him under the chin. "Did you have a good day?"

"Ruff!" *Yes!*

"Pru, you'll never guess what I found out!" Martha hollered from the living room. "Come inside so I can tell you!"

She hurried into the living room, and sank down on the yellow sofa next to Martha.

"Well?"

"You don't look so good." Martha eyed her frankly. "Maybe you'd better tell me what happened today."

She did, first mentioning Kevin, and then enjoying the outraged expression on her friend's face when she told her about Bridget asking –

or had it been demanding? – a job at the library.

"No!" Martha's mouth fell open. "Well, she's got nerve, I'll give her that. Huh. Maybe I should write her in as a character in my retired lady detective script. Not this one because I don't know where I could stick her in, but in the next one she could be the villain – or a criminal – or the—"

"You're going to write a second episode?"

"Maybe." Martha nodded. "That's another thing I was going to tell you. See, my agent called wanting to know how was I coming along with my script. They're still not making any more princess movies which is a poop, because my agent said she liked my script for that, but now she's just heard a whisper she called it, of a new TV producer wanting to make a crime show and she wants me to send her my retired lady detective. Except I haven't finished it." Martha pouted.

"Can you email her what you've written so far?"

"Yeah, she said to do that, and she'll read it right away. But how am I going to finish it in the next couple of weeks when it's taken me months to get this far with it? And we have to solve Sunny's murder as well!"

"We could let Mitch solve Sunny's case," Pru pointed out gently.

"But where's the fun in that?" Martha's pout deepened.

"Wouldn't you like to see your retired lady detective on TV?"

"You bet I would!" Martha brightened. "You're right, Pru. I can do both! After all, I *am* retired. And if I stay home and work on my script instead of going to the senior center or the café – although I'll miss visiting with the girls and Annie, and so will Teddy – I can write in the morning and sleuth in the afternoon!"

"That wasn't quite what I meant—"

"Lemme tell you what I found out today. First, AJ, that's Ed's cat, wants to join the toy exchange." A hungry expression flitted across

Martha's face. "We should get some of his Danishes next time at the café. Except he doesn't work Saturdays. And I found out who's friends with Danielle's grandmother!"

"That's great news," Pru replied.

"Yeah, now we can question her!"

"What about? I'm sure she didn't kill Sunny."

"Probably not, but we might be able to find out more about Danielle, who *is* one of our suspects. I think today took more out of you than usual." Martha eyed her critically. "Where's your sleuthing power?"

"You're right." Her stomach rumbled which reminded her … "What do you think about having an emergency pizza night?"

"Goody." Martha grinned. "That's another piece of good news! Yeah! Let's have pepperoni – no, Hawaiian – no, a Lauren special – no, a—"

"What about mushroom, sausage, and pineapple?"

Martha' s eyes widened. "That's a weird combination, but yeah, why not?"

"Ruff!" Teddy climbed onto the sofa and placed his head on Martha's lap.

"I wish you could have some, little guy, but it might make you sick. You'll have your own special dinner."

Teddy made a low noise which indicated he wasn't convinced.

"What about one of your special treat cookies?" Pru suggested.

At the word treat, Teddy's gaze lifted toward her and he looked hopeful.

"Yeah, you get a treat with Pru," Martha encouraged. "And then we need to update our suspect list. Put Kevin right at the top of the list, and add Danielle's grandma's friend. And then after pizza tonight, I'll start working on my script!"

CHAPTER 11

The next morning, Martha practically stumbled to the breakfast table, pushing her walker.

"Whew!" She plopped down in the chair and looked at Pru with bleary eyes. "I gotta tell you, I'm not as young as I used to be."

"Did you work on your script a long time?"

"You betcha!" Martha nodded. "And I got a lot done, if I do say so myself. But maybe I'd better read it later today, in case some of it doesn't make sense."

"I understand." Martha's late night made her think about studying hard at college.

"And when you get home from work, we can visit Danielle's grandmother's friend."

"What's her name?"

"Judith. She doesn't live too far from here, so we could walk, and Teddy can come."

"Ruff!" Teddy appeared, carrying a slightly faded blue giraffe. He dropped it at Pru's feet.

"What's this?" She gently picked it up and examined it. "Is this for me?"

Teddy shook his head.

"For the toy exchange?" she guessed.

"Ruff!" *Yes!*

"Isn't that sweet?" Martha gazed at her fur baby in approval. "What a good boy you are, Teddy. We can take this giraffe to the café today."

"I thought you were going to work on your script in the mornings," Pru said.

"But I got a lot of work done last night, so I can take this morning off." Martha waved her hand in the air. "And instead of a hot chocolate there, I might need a latte – maybe one with a double shot – on account of my late night. And maybe a cupcake – or one of Ed's Danishes."

"I see." Pru fought the temptation to smile.

"And this afternoon when you get home from the library we can go sleuthing," Martha continued. "So I could work on my script after lunch – if I wanted to."

"Ruff!" *Yes!*

"And you need to start thinking if you want to hold the yoga class again this week, on account of it being Thursday today. I can make more posters for you on the weekend."

"Thanks, but—"

"Maybe those two ladies will come back," Martha continued. "You know, the ones we didn't know who might have been friends with Danielle."

"One of them definitely was." Pru remembered the woman accosting her in the library and accusing her of not doing boat or camel pose.

"If you teach another class, you might lure them back here."

"Are you going to use that word, *lure*, in your script?" Martha had been using it a little lately.

"I already have – last night." Martha chuckled. "It's a good word, isn't it?"

"It is," she agreed.

"And maybe Jesse will come to your yoga class too – so make sure you wear your lipstick next time."

"I haven't decided whether to hold another class," she protested.

"I bet everyone will come again," Martha continued, as if she hadn't heard Pru. "Zoe, Lauren, Doris, Brooke, Claire. That's five people already and if you don't want to do it for the money, you can give all the cash to Father Mike again."

"I might just do that," she murmured.

"Ooh – maybe Danielle will come to the next one! I'll make sure we tell Judith about it, so she'll tell Danielle's grandma."

***

To Pru's relief, there was no sight of Bridget that day at the library. Hopefully she'd gotten the message after Barbara's dismissal.

What sort of questions would they ask Danielle's grandmother's friend Judith? She wondered if Danielle would actually come to her next yoga class – if she held one. Pru was still undecided.

By the time the clock struck four, she couldn't wait to get home and talk over sleuthing strategy with Martha and Teddy.

"I'm a good girl," Martha greeted her cheerfully in the hall, wearing purple sweatpants and matching sweater. "We went to the café this morning, didn't we, Teddy, and then after lunch I got straight to work on my retired lady detective."

"Ruff!"

"That's great." Pru smiled, following Martha down the hall and into the living room.

"So now we've gotta visit Judith. She lives near the park." Martha looked at her expectantly.

"This very minute?"

"Ruff!" Teddy shifted impatiently, standing next to her.

"Grab a glass of water first if you want," Martha said, wheeling her walker around to face the hall, "and then we can go. It's my turn to cook tonight and I'm making corned beef hash."

"Yum." Pru quickly filled a glass of water and downed it, then joined Martha and Teddy in the hall. "How far away is Judith's house?"

"Only a few minutes' drive." Martha waved her hand in the air. "I'm going to ask her all about Danielle, and how she knows her grandmother."

"Good thinking."

"And I sent my partly finished retired lady detective script off to my agent today as well." Martha sounded pleased with herself. "She said she's gonna read it tonight."

"Ruff!" *Goody!*

Pru placed Martha's walker in the trunk of her small SUV, and they drove off down the road lined with Victorian-era houses.

"Turn left. Then right. Then left again," Martha instructed.

When they drove toward the park, Teddy gave a high-pitched bark.

Martha and Pru looked at each other.

"Uh-oh," Martha said. "I think that's Teddy's *I gotta go* bark."

Pru parked at the curb. "I'll take him."

"I'll come, too. Stretch my legs. We can walk to Judith's house from here anyway – it's just down the road."

"Okay." Pru got out Martha's walker, and gathered Teddy's lead. "I should have a poo bag in my purse."

"Good thinking." Martha flipped open the seat of her walker and rummaged around. "I'm out of them."

"Ruff!" Teddy jiggled on the spot.

"Let's go." Pru led Teddy onto the grassy expanse of lawn. The park was deserted, even the small swing set at the opposite end.

"I'll catch up with you," Martha called, trundling behind them.

After Teddy finished, and Pru was glad that a poo bag was *not* necessary, she noticed a strange shape out of the corner of her eye. It was at the far corner of the park. Was it a rock? She passed the small boulder she had hidden behind a few months ago in acting out one of the scenes from Martha's script.

Was it a piece of wood? She squinted, but couldn't make anything out apart from a glimpse of blue and green.

Her eyes widened. Bridget had worn those colors the first time she'd visited the library.

"Ruff?" Teddy looked up at her, his brown button eyes questioning.

"Martha!" She turned and waved to her. "I'm going to look at something over here." She pointed. "You stay there."

"Ooh, what is it?" Martha sped up, wheeling the walker like a pro.

"I think it might be—"

"Ruff! Ruff!" Teddy strained against the leash, suddenly wanting to investigate.

"Hold on, little guy. Pru will take you over there. Don't get yourself—"

"Ruff! Ruff!"

Pru had no option but to allow Teddy to tow her forward – fast. Her heart raced as they approached the strange object. Surely it wouldn't be

141

anything sinister? Perhaps it was just an old sweater someone had tossed away.

But as they approached, she felt a little sick. It looked more and more like a person lying on the ground, dressed in the same outfit Bridget had worn recently – blue jeans and a green T-shirt.

"Ruff!" Teddy sat down next to Bridget. She sprawled on the ground, face down. A bloody gash on the back of her head was the reason.

CHAPTER 12

Was it really Bridget? Maybe it was someone dressed in the same outfit but who was a totally different person. But the wavy caramel hair looked just like hers. Pru crept towards the person's profile, her heart sinking. It *was* Bridget. Her sightless eye stared at the dirt and grass.

"Who is it?" Martha asked breathlessly, reaching them. She scanned Pru's expression. "Uh-oh. You don't look too good."

"It's Bridget."

"Your Bridget? Lemme see." She pushed her walker over to the girl's body. "Yeah, it's her. I think."

"I'm sure it's her," Pru said in a small voice.

"I'm sorry." Martha patted her shoulder. "I'll call Mitch. Do you want to sit on my walker seat? You look like you need to."

"I'll be okay," she replied. "You sit down."

"Well, if you're sure." Martha plonked down on the black vinyl padded seat and turned on her phone. After talking to Mitch for a minute, she ended the call.

"He's sending someone," Martha told her. "He's tied up on something else so he's sending—"

"Jesse?"

"Yeah."

Now she really felt like sitting down on Martha's walker.

"When was the last time you saw Bridget?" Martha asked.

"At the library yesterday," she replied. "After Barbara told her she wasn't hiring, she left."

"Huh." Martha looked like she was pondering. When she finally spoke, she said, "This puts a whole new spin on our investigation. Why would someone kill Bridget? She's not even from around here. So why would someone have a beef with her? She's only been in town how long?"

"I'm not sure, but I guess the police can check with the local motel when she booked a room there."

"Good thinking." Martha nodded in approval.

"Ruff!" Teddy sat in front of Pru's feet and glanced up at her, as if he sensed she was distressed.

"Thanks," she whispered, scratching him behind the ears.

The sound of a vehicle approaching made her look up – police.

Her heart sank when a familiar figure strode towards them – Jesse. He wore black slacks and a subtly checked blue shirt.

"Mitch told me you discovered someone," he said.

"Bridget," she murmured.

"Bridget? The girl from your yoga class?" His expression sharpened.

"That's her," Martha told him.

"The paramedics should be here any minute," he said. "I'll check her now, though."

A minute later, he rejoined them. "She's gone." He took a notepad out of his pocket. "How did you find her?"

Pru told him, all the while thinking it wouldn't be long before Jesse found out about the cheating scandal. She'd wondered if – when – she would tell him one day, and now it looked like that decision had been taken out of her hands. By Bridget. Or more accurately – Bridget's killer.

A range of emotions ran through her – sorrow, anger, shock. Why would someone want to kill Bridget? Who even knew she was in town? She said she'd been just passing through at Sunny's yoga class before she hit up Pru for a job at the library. For a moment she had the sudden urge to laugh. What if Barbara had killed Bridget for having the nerve to ask her for a position?

Noticing Martha was standing now, she abruptly sank onto the walker seat.

"Did either of you touch anything?" Jesse wanted to know, looking keenly at Pru.

"No." She thought back. "No," she said more definitely. "Teddy sat next to her, though."

"When was the last time you saw her?"

Pru told him about Bridget turning up at the library yesterday and asking Barbara for a job.

"I'll have to confirm that with Barbara."

"Oh no," Pru blurted.

"Why?"

"Just – you know – boss employee politics."

"I get it." He nodded. "Don't worry."

"What if Barbara thinks I did it?" Pru blurted.

"Did you?" He looked at her keenly.

"Jesse!" Martha sounded shocked. "How could you? Pru's a good girl – of course she didn't kill Bridget, even though she had reason to. I mean – oops." Martha realized what'd she just blabbed and closed her lips firmly. "Sorry, Pru," she murmured out of the side of her mouth.

"Ruff!" Teddy said in a scolding tone to Martha.

"You're right, little guy." Martha nodded. "I shouldn't have said anything at all."

"Would you like to tell me what's going on?" Jesse raised an eyebrow. "Just how well did you know Bridget?"

"It's a long story," Pru said.

"I've got plenty of time."

Pru took a deep breath, and told him all of it. How Bridget had used her to cheat in college, how Pru had nearly been expelled although she hadn't done anything wrong, how she'd found it almost impossible to get a job until she'd snagged the position at the Gold Leaf Valley library, the only offer she'd received.

"Don't forget to tell him about the loudmouthed receptionist at the college who told prospective employers all about it," Martha advised.

"And then Bridget turned up here," Pru said a short while later. "At Sunny's yoga class. She said she was just passing through on a cross-country trip. And then she showed up at the library and asked me for a job."

"As if Pru could hire her." Martha snorted.

"And then she asked Barbara for a job yesterday, which I already mentioned."

"Anything else?" Jesse asked after a moment.

"No." Pru shook her head. "I think that's all."

"That's plenty, isn't it?" Martha asked.

"It looks like there's enough to go on for the moment," Jesse conceded. "I'll check with the motel and find out when Bridget first registered."

"That's what Pru said you'd probably do," Martha sounded pleased.

"Got any more tips for me?" Jesse asked Pru good-naturedly.

"No." She looked up at him, wondering if he would judge her for being caught up in Bridget's cheating scandal. So far, his manner toward her hadn't changed. But would it, once he processed everything she'd just told him? Suddenly, it was very important to her that it didn't.

"What's wrong?" He frowned.

"Nothing."

Just then, the paramedics arrived.

"Ooh, there's Chris." Martha pointed to a tall man with even, attractive features, who was married to Zoe.

"I'll be back in a minute." Jesse strode over to Chris and spoke to him.

Pru watched Chris reply, and then he and his crew member approached Bridget's body.

"You two – three—" Jesse glanced down at Teddy, who sniffed his shoes "—better go home. I'll stop by if I have any follow up questions."

"Does this mean you're in charge of the investigation?" Martha wanted to know. "Or is Mitch going to take over?"

"Mitch is busy with Sunny's death, among other things," Jesse replied. "I *have* investigated murders before, you know. In Sacramento. Mitch and

I will discuss both cases and see if they're linked."

"This might be a toughie for the senior sleuthing club." Martha's eyes glinted with determination. "But we're ready for the task!"

"I hope you're not," Jesse replied. "Please, ladies – and Teddy—" he glanced down at the Coton still sniffing his shoes "—leave this matter to the police."

"We'll see," Martha replied. "Come on, Pru, we can still visit Judith – that's allowed, right, Jesse? We can visit our friends?"

"Yes, but please don't mention finding Bridget's body – not yet, anyway," he replied.

"Well, pooh." Martha wrinkled her nose. "Okay, I'll try, but I bet it's all right once she's on the news."

"Yes," Jesse replied a touch wearily.

"Gotta go!" Martha grabbed the handles of her walker. "Let's roll, Pru."

With a little backward glance at Jesse, she followed Martha, Teddy trotting at her side.

"We're still visiting Judith." Martha puffed slightly as they neared the car. "But maybe we'd better drive the rest of the way on account of all this walking we've just done."

"Good idea." Pru stowed the walker in the trunk and drove the few yards down the road to a little blue Victorian-era house with white trim.

"Are you okay?" She looked at her friend in concern once she parked. Martha's cheeks were pale and she'd closed her eyes briefly.

"I'm fine." Martha waved away her concern. "Today turned out to be busier than I expected, what with my café visit this morning, working on my script, and now finding another dead body – sorry – Bridget. And now we've got to question Judith about Danielle's grandmother."

"We can do it another day if you'd like."

"No, we're here now, so we might as well talk to Judith right away." Martha clambered out of the SUV.

Pru followed, grabbing the walker and letting Teddy out of the car.

"Ruff?" Teddy looked at the small garden, covered in riots of flowers – blue, pink, orange, and red.

"Yeah, this is a good garden," Martha agreed. "Maybe I can ask her for some gardening tips once we get the sleuthing stuff out of the way."

"Any plants would need to be dog safe," Pru reminded her.

"That's important." Martha nodded. She started up the little path to the front door and said over her shoulder, "I might not cook tonight, after all. Maybe we'd better order pizza again."

"I could cook," she offered instantly.

"You're a good girl, but you'll be tired too when we get home," Martha replied. "If we have pizza again tonight we can be extra good and not have it at all next week."

"Okay." The thought of cooking didn't really appeal to her right now after discovering Bridget, but she was conscious of Martha's age and tried to pick up the slack when she could.

"You choose the toppings," Pru offered.

"Yeah." Martha grinned, then turned toward the white front door again.

After knocking, they heard footsteps walking towards the door.

"Why, Martha!" A tall, elderly lady with snowy hair looked at her in surprise. "What on earth are you doing here? I mean, come in."

"Thanks, Judith." Martha wheeled her walker into the hall.

"And who's this little one?" Judith bent down to say hello to Teddy.

"Ruff!" *I'm Teddy!*

"This is Teddy. And Pru." Martha remembered her manners.

"What can I do for all of you?" Judith asked. "He is just the cutest thing, Martha, just like you told us." She glanced down at Teddy again.

"Thanks." Martha grinned. "I'm so glad Ed told me about him – he was waiting at the animal shelter for a forever home."

"And you found him." Judith nodded.

"Pru works at the library,' Martha continued. "So if you ever need to find a book, ask her. One day she'll be the head honcho there and probably in charge of all the libraries in California! She really knows books."

Pru felt herself blushing a little at Martha's lavish praise.

"I'll remember." Judith smiled at Pru. "How nice to work in a library."

"It is," she agreed. Most of the time, anyway.

"Come and sit." Judith ushered them into the small living room decorated in shades of cream and periwinkle. "Now, can I get you a cup of coffee? Or hot chocolate? I think I have a box of the stuff stashed away somewhere. Or juice?"

"Thanks, but we won't bother you." Martha waved a hand in the air. "We came to ask you about Danielle's grandmother."

"Sheila?"

"Yeah, if that's her name." Martha nodded. "See, Danielle was in the yoga class before Sunny the instructor was killed. And then Pru held her own yoga class but Danielle didn't come. So Pru is thinking of holding another class next week and we don't want Danielle to miss out. We know how she is about her yoga."

Pru stared at Martha. She didn't remember Martha mentioning this line of questioning.

"Oh, yes, yoga is just about all Danielle talks about." Judith chuckled. "That's what Sheila says, anyway. So when I saw the poster about Pru's yoga class, I told Sheila about it, and she said she'd tell Danielle. But she didn't come?" She turned to Pru.

Pru shifted on the periwinkle sofa. "I found out later she was attending another yoga class," she finally said.

"Yeah, it's too bad both classes were on at the same time." Martha pouted. "But anyway, we just wanted to make sure Danielle knows about Pru's next class, in case she wants to attend. And we don't know how else to get in touch with her."

"That's very thoughtful of you, Martha." Judith smiled. "Don't worry, I'll call Sheila tonight and tell her. Is it at Father Mike's church hall again, dear?" She turned to Pru.

"That's right," Pru replied, wondering what she – or Martha – had gotten her into.

"Ruff!" Teddy agreed.

"Teddy was there, too," Martha told Judith.

"He was a big help," Pru added, remembering how the Coton had assisted in taking the money and making the payment part fun instead of awkward.

"That's lovely." Judith smiled at Teddy.

Teddy seemed to return her smile, showing his white teeth in what Pru was sure was a sweet doggy grin.

Martha and Judith chatted for a few minutes about the upcoming classes at the senior center, including watercolor painting and scrabble, and then Martha stood.

"We'd better get going." She wrapped her fingers around the walker handles. "We've had a busy day and I've got to work on my script this weekend."

"Oh, your retired lady detective?" Judith sounded interested.

"You've heard about it?"

"Someone told me at the senior center. They said you talked about it a lot a few months ago but haven't heard you mention it lately."

"Yeah, all that talk was fun, but then I actually had to write down all my ideas." Martha tapped her head. "But now I've really got to step it up – I'll tell you if I get some good news about it all."

"Oh, that does sound exciting." Judith ushered them out. 'I wish I was as creative as you, Martha."

"But your garden is beautiful." Pru spoke. "Did you do all the work?"

"Yes, I did, and chose all the different flowers and colors." Judith sounded proud. "Thank you, dear. It does give me pleasure when I come home to see all the different varieties, as if they're welcoming me back."

"I'm sure they are," Pru replied.

"Ruff!"

They said goodbye to Judith and started down the path.

"See, you *are* going to be a head honcho one day because you notice things like this." Martha pointed to the flowers lining the path. "And then you talk about them. I need to copy you because I forgot to ask her about the garden."

"I meant what I said," Pru replied.

"I know." Martha nodded earnestly. "And that's what makes you a good girl."

CHAPTER 13

That night, Martha chose pepperoni and pineapple for their pizza. It had turned out to be one of their favorites.

"Ruff?" Teddy sat next to Martha' chair, looking wryly hopeful.

"Pepperoni isn't good for you, little guy," Martha told him sadly. "I'm sorry."

"How about a dog cookie?" Pru rose, leaving her half-eaten slice on her plate.

"Ruff!" *Yes!*

"You spoil him just like me." Martha chuckled. "But you've been a good boy today, Teddy, like you always are, so it's only right you get a treat. Thanks." She turned to Pru expectantly.

After giving Teddy a pumpkin and cheese cookie from the special jar, Pru took her seat again at the kitchen table and dug into her slice. She was glad Martha had suggested pizza again.

"So what do we do now?" she asked after finishing her second piece. "With the sleuthing?"

"We're gonna have to check our list of suspects," Martha told her. "Now we've got two murders to solve – Sunny's and Bridget's. What if they're linked?"

"How could they be?" Pru frowned, still feeling shell-shocked over Bridget's death. She'd actually *known* her. What would Bridget's family think when they found out – would they consider that Pru might have killed her? It would look like a strange coincidence to anyone that Bridget had turned up in the same small town that Pru had moved to, and ended up murdered a short while later.

"I don't know," Martha admitted. She peered at Pru. "Are you okay? You don't look so good."

"What if everyone thinks I killed Bridget?"

"Huh." Martha sat back in her chair. "I hadn't thought of that. Yeah, they might."

"Martha." Her voice was strangled.

"I know you didn't do it," Martha replied.

"Ruff!" *Me too!*

"Jesse and Mitch will know you didn't – well, they should," Martha amended. "And all your friends here will know you didn't. You're too nice to kill anyone."

"Thanks. Should I call home and tell them what's happened?" Pru crinkled her brow. "Or should I wait until Jesse has a chance to tell Bridget's parents?"

"That's a good idea." Martha nodded. "Wait until tomorrow. I'm guessing he might have already told them by now. Anyway, your folks know you're living here with me – us—" she looked down at Teddy who sat next to her chair, "—and have your cell phone number."

"And yours." She'd given it to her parents in case of emergencies.

"So if they need to talk to you, they will."

Pru allowed herself to be content with that. Maybe she could call Jesse and ask if he'd broken the news to Bridget's family yet? No, she didn't want to bother him – not tonight, anyway.

They cleared the dishes away and sat back down at the table.

"Where's our suspect list?" Martha felt in her pockets of her sweatpants.

"Maybe it's in the living room." Pru hurried in there, grabbed the list from the coffee table and returned.

"We've got Kevin, Angela, Danielle, those two ladies who attended your yoga class and – who else?" Martha tapped the pen on the table.

"But why would any of those people kill Bridget?"

"Good question." Martha nodded. "Ooh – Barbara!"

Pru stared at her. "Are you a mind reader? I thought that for an instant when I found Bridget's bo – Bridget."

"It sounds like Bridget definitely annoyed Barb," Martha said.

"Barbara."

"That's what I said."

"If you ever meet her again, I think you should know she only likes being called by her full name – Barbara."

"Okay," Martha said after a moment. "I don't want to make things awkward for you at the library. And some people don't like the nicknames other people give them. Good point."

"Ruff!" Teddy stretched up to Martha on his hind legs.

"Do you want to sit at the table, too?" Martha bent down to pick him up.

"Let me." Pru gently held him and placed him on the chair next to Martha. "How's that?"

"Ruff!" *Good!*

"I'm gonna write down Barbara." Martha did so. "Now, who else?"

"Who else is there?" Pru looked at her. "Unless we try and find anyone Bridget interacted with while she was here. Like Paul, the motel owner—"

"Good one!" Martha wrote down his name.

"But why would he kill Bridget? Unless she was late paying for her room? But why would he kill her over that? All he has to do is charge her credit card – he must have put it on file when she turned up there. I mean, that's what he did when I stayed there."

"Like I said to Jesse, this is a toughie. How are we going to find out who Bridget chatted to while she was here? Besides, you, Jesse at yoga, and Barbara."

"Everyone at Sunny's yoga class," Pru said reluctantly.

"Yeah!" Martha's eyes lit up. "You, Doris, Zoe, Danielle, and who else was there?"

"Not Lauren," she replied thinking back. "The two ladies who came to my yoga class. They might have attended Sunny's session – they looked vaguely familiar."

"Ooh – I've just had a thought!" Martha sounded delighted. "I bet it's

Kevin – what if Bridget tried to rent an apartment from him?"

"That's a good idea," Pru said. "But do you know if he has any rentals? Or is it all storefronts?"

"We've gotta find out!" Martha made a note, then yawned. "All this sleuthing is making me tired. Tomorrow I should hear back from my agent about my retired lady detective script, and then we can hold another meeting and think up some more suspects."

"What about going to the café?" she suggested.

"Ruff!"

"We can give Teddy's blue giraffe to the toy exchange. You never know, we might pick up some more gossip tomorrow morning!"

CHAPTER 14

Pru's phone buzzed early the next morning. It was her mother. She must have heard the news about Bridget.

"Yes, I'm fine," she assured her. After telling her mom in brief detail about discovering Bridget at the park, and promising to be very careful, she ended the call on a lighter note, mentioning their visit to the café that morning.

She'd just sat down at the kitchen table, looking forward to her breakfast, although it was flavorless fiber cereal, when Martha's phone sounded.

"Ooh!" Martha turned from the toaster to grab her phone from her walker basket. "It's her!" She looked up from the screen. "My agent!"

"Ruff!" Teddy danced around Martha's feet, then sat, looking at the phone expectantly.

"Good boy," Martha said. "You know not to trip me up."

"Wuff."

"Answer it," Pru urged, hoping it was good news.

Martha spoke into the phone. "You did? And? Really? Uh-huh. Yeah, I'll get right on it. Okay, thanks!" Martha ended the call and grinned at Pru. "She loves it!"

"Really?"

"Yep! And she wants me to finish it quickly so she can send it to the TV producer."

"I guess you'll be busy this weekend, then."

"Yeah, but I can still fit in a trip to the café this morning," Martha said. "And we can try and find out more about Kevin – maybe Lauren and Zoe know something about him. And then this afternoon I'll work on my script and we can hold another suspect meeting. Hmm." She scrunched up her face. "I still wanna work that tree pose of yours into my script, but it might have to wait until the second episode. Ooh – I know!

You can give this Bridget girl a boost doing tree pose and then fall down because you've lost your balance, and she falls down too, but she's the one who gets caught, not you. Yeah!"

"You've got a plot for the second episode already?" Pru stared at her.

"Nope. That just came to me." Martha chuckled. "Because I'm a writer now. I'll jot that down though, so I don't forget. It sounds good."

"It does."

"And then you can get your revenge on Bridget that way." Martha sounded gleeful. "Not that I'm happy that someone killed her, although it sounds like she might have done something to someone to make them mad enough to murder her. Not you," she added hastily. "But someone. Otherwise, why would she be dead?"

***

Pru enjoyed her visit to the café, although they lingered a little too long on the manner of Bridget's death for her liking. Lauren and Zoe told them it had been on the TV news the previous night.

After giving Lauren and Zoe Teddy's contribution to the toy exchange, as well as returning the pink ball Mrs. Snuggle gave Teddy, she was delighted to receive a soft mouse from AJ.

"I bet Teddy will like playing with that," Martha observed as Pru tucked it into the walker basket.

"Ruff!" *Yes!* He sat next to Annie at the table.

Lauren and Zoe both promised to come to Pru's next yoga class.

"I wonder if Jesse will turn up again." Zoe giggled.

Pru couldn't help blushing a little.

"He'll be dumb if he doesn't," Martha stated.

"Ruff!"

***

"I'm making Kevin our main suspect," Martha told her on the short drive home from the café. "The girls haven't heard of him owning any apartments or houses, but what if he had a secret one stashed away and promised to rent it to Bridget and then he got angry and smashed a rock on her head?"

"But why would he do that?" Pru asked.

"Because she wanted a lower rent and threatened to report him if he didn't give it to her? If he's doing it off the books and not reporting his income, it might be worth killing her over."

"Do you know any of this or it is just supposition?" Once more, she marveled at Martha's theories. Maybe her retired lady detective script would be a big hit.

"I'm just guessing," Martha admitted. "But it makes sense, doesn't it?"

"Unfortunately it does," she agreed.

"Ruff!"

"So when we get home we can have lunch, and then I'll work on my script. And after that, we can visit

Kevin and ask him some questions!"
Martha's eyes lit up.

"All that won't be too tiring for you,
will it?" Pru asked.

"Ruff?" Teddy added.

"Don't worry about me," Martha
replied. "I'll be fine. All this sleuthing
gives me energy. Plus, I'm excited
again about my retired lady
detective. Just imagine if they *do*
make it into a TV show!"

"That would be amazing!"

"Ruff!" *Yes!*

After a quick lunch, Martha retired
to her bedroom to work on her script,
while Pru relaxed on the sofa reading
a mystery from the library. Teddy sat
beside her. It was a classic Agatha
Christie and she was enjoying the
characters of Tommy and Tuppence.

She was so engrossed in the story
that at first she didn't hear Martha
enter the living area.

"I said, are you ready to visit
Kevin?"

"Have you finished your script
already?" Pru placed her leather
bookmark into the novel.

"Nearly," Martha said proudly. "Having this kind of deadline really puts a fire under me. Maybe my agent should give me a deadline for every script. I just have to finish it off and it might be all ready for tomorrow!"

"What about typos?" Pru asked suspiciously. She'd peeked at Martha's typing a while ago and it had been littered with the dreaded errors.

"Yeah, I've gotta fix those up, too. So maybe it will be one hundred percent ready tomorrow night. My agent's a nice gal, but she's not too understanding about those typos."

After snapping on Teddy's leash, Pru was ready to sleuth.

"Where does Kevin live?"

"I don't know," Martha admitted. "But the girls said he visits his mom on the weekends to do some work in the yard for her. Which is a nice thing to do. Huh. So maybe he isn't the killer."

"I think killers can have more than one aspect to their personality," Pru mused.

"You're right," Martha agreed. "Look at the ones we've nabbed so far."

"Two?"

"Two is better than none. And no way did I think those people were killers originally. So Kevin could still be our man."

"I hope you know where his mother lives."

"I do." Martha nodded. "It's not far from the café. We can drive there."

"Okay." Pru hustled them into her small SUV and they set off, Martha giving her the directions.

Before long they pulled up outside a slightly ramshackle, olive Victorian cottage.

"The windows look a bit warped," Martha observed, unfastening her seatbelt.

"They do." Pru retrieved the walker from the trunk and helped Teddy out of the car. "What do we do if Kevin – oh, look, I think that's him!" She pointed to a figure kneeling at the side of the garden.

"Goody." Martha grinned. "Follow my lead. Yoo hoo, Kevin!" She charged forward with her walker, opening the little gate and entering the garden.

The figure straightened, stood, and turned to look at Martha, his eyes widening.

"Yes?" he asked a little suspiciously.

"I'm Martha, and this is Pru and Teddy." Martha pointed to them hurrying after her.

"You're from the library." Kevin gestured to Pru.

"That's right," she replied.

"Ruff!" Teddy sniffed his boots for a second, then trotted back to Martha and Pru.

"That bogus system hasn't given me another overdue fine, has it?" He frowned.

"No, it's nothing like that," she assured him.

"Then why are you—"

"We wanted to know if you have any houses to rent," Martha said. "See, Pru's brothers are coming out here and they need somewhere to live, but my place is too small for them. I'm practically bursting at the seams already with Pru and Teddy, but we're a good combo."

Pru blinked, wondering how Martha came up with all this on the spur of the moment. Or had she been thinking it up on the drive over?

"I see." He relaxed a little. "Unfortunately, I don't have any rentals like that."

"Not even for a girl called Bridget?" Martha winked at him.

He leaned back. "I don't know who you're talking about. I wish I did have living quarters to rent – what with housing hard to find in this town, I'd make some good money. But I still have the space Sunny rented from me, and now it's ready to lease again." He looked at Pru hopefully. "It's a great place to hold a yoga class. If the church hall gets booked up, you can rent that instead."

"Thanks, but I've already booked the hall for next week again."

"How much are you paying?" he asked.

"Ten dollars."

"I can't beat that." He sounded disappointed. "What about your yoga friends? Maybe they want to hold classes at my studio."

"I'm teaching mostly beginners," she replied.

"Since Sunny died, I can't find anyone else to rent it," he said morosely.

"But she only died very recently," Martha said.

"Yeah, and her death has been all over the news, so there aren't any takers." He blew out a gusty breath. "Once again, Sunny has screwed me over. Even in her death."

"Well, thanks for talking to us," Martha said briskly. "We'll be on our way."

"Let me know if you change your mind about the studio space," Kevin called after them.

"I don't think he's the killer but I didn't like the way he kept wanting you to hire his studio," Martha spoke out of the side of her mouth as they walked back to the car.

"Ruff!"

"Me neither – to both," Pru replied.

"I don't think he was lying when he said he didn't know who Bridget was."

"I don't think he was her type. So I can't imagine her meeting him in a bar and being interested." Pru froze when she opened the car door. "Is there a bar here?"

"Good question. Yeah, there is one past the senior center, but I've never been there. We can go if you want."

"I don't want to, really," she said. That had never been her scene.

"Me neither," Martha admitted. "Maybe we should just go home. We can go over our suspect list again and cross Kevin off it and plan our next move!"

CHAPTER 15

That night at dinner, over chicken pot pie that Pru made, Martha said, "We should visit the motel and ask to see Bridget's room. That's what they do in all the crime TV shows."

"What are we looking for?"

"Ruff?"

"A clue. Or something that will point us in the next direction." Martha waved a pie-laden fork at Pru. "We could ask Paul, the motel owner, if Bridget mentioned going to the bar. Maybe we should have gone there today just to be thorough, but—"

"I know what you mean." Pru nodded.

"Not that it's a dive or anything like that," Martha added. "Some of the men at the senior center mention it occasionally and they're respectable people. Ooh – what if you call Jesse and ask him if he's checked out the bar?"

"Why don't you?"

"Because I'm sure he'd rather hear from you than me." Martha chuckled. "If you don't want to, I can call Mitch instead."

"I'd prefer not to call him," Pru said. She hadn't seen Jesse since she'd stumbled across Bridget's body. Now that he was aware of her past, she didn't know what his attitude toward her would be when they ran across each other again. Maybe she didn't want to know. But that was being a coward.

"Okay, I can do it." Martha rummaged in her walker basket for her phone.

"Martha! You can't disturb Mitch on a Saturday night."

"But he might be working. Sometimes he works on the weekend, especially when he's trying to solve a murder. And it's not even seven yet." She looked up and peered at the large kitchen clock on the wall. "He's probably not even sitting down to his dinner."

"I still don't think—"

But Martha had already dialed. "Hey, Mitch, did you check the bar to see if Bridget visited it? It's me, Martha. She might have bumped into a Kevin there – you know, the guy who owns the studio where Sunny was killed?"

There was a short pause. Pru felt like resting her head in her hands.

"Jesse's looking into that? Then I'll get Pru to give him a call and get the info. Uh-huh. He is? I'll let her know. Thanks."

"Well?" Pru looked at her expectantly.

"He's all yours. Jesse. Mitch said it's his night off, and he was the one asking questions at the bar. So you'd better give him a call."

She just stared at Martha. "What? No, I couldn't. I don't want to disturb him."

"Not even for the senior sleuthing club?" Martha batted her eyelashes.

"Ruff?"

"See, Teddy wants you to."

She looked down at Teddy, who sat next to her chair, looking hopeful. "Maybe Teddy can call Jesse."

"Ha! Good one." Martha chortled. "I bet he could if he wanted to, though. I know Annie can call people on the phone and she talks Norwegian Forest Cat to them. Lauren told me."

"Really?"

"Yep," Martha replied proudly. "I bet Annie can teach Teddy how to do it – except not the Norwegian Forest talking bit. But Teddy can talk Coton instead."

"Ruff!" Teddy looked pleased at being spoken about.

"I bet he could." Pru smiled and scratched him behind the ears.

"So tomorrow we'll go to church, and afterwards go to the motel and check it out. Then after lunch I'll have to work on my retired lady."

"Okay," she agreed.

Martha shut herself away with her script while Pru and Teddy watched a spy drama on TV. She couldn't help thinking it wasn't the same watching it on her own now –

sometimes Martha made comments that were fun to hear, instead of annoying.

When she finally decided to go to bed, it was just after ten. Knocking on Martha's bedroom door, she called, "Martha? Are you okay?"

"Ruff!" Teddy stretched up and scratched on the closed wooden door.

"I'm fine," Martha hollered. "You can send Teddy in. I'm almost done for tonight. Those pesky typos are nearly all gone – I think."

"Okay." Pru opened the door and Teddy scampered in. "Good night."

"Night," Martha called. "Get ready for sleuthing tomorrow!"

***

The next morning after church, they headed to the motel.

Red roses adorned the front garden, along with a lush, green lawn. Although the Swiss chalet style building could use a coat of paint, the owner maintained the grounds nicely.

"Hey." Martha nudged Pru in the ribs as they parked in the lot. "You didn't call Jesse last night about his bar investigation – did you?"

"I forgot," she replied truthfully. She'd remembered early that morning when she briefly woke, then dropped back to sleep.

"You can do it now." Martha's eyes lit up.

"But we're at the motel."

"I'd do it but my phone is in my walker basket, which is in the trunk."

"Fine." Pru sighed and pulled her phone out of her purse. And dialed. "What am I going to say to him?" She wasn't going to admit that her stomach had started fluttering.

"If he found out if Bridget visited the bar – and met Kevin there."

"Right." Why did this feel like she was twelve years old and calling a boy for the first time?

When Jesse answered, her mind went blank for a second. "Um … the bar – Bridget – did you find out—"

"Pru?"

"Yes, it's Pru." She frowned at the phone.

"Tell him we want to know if Bridget went to the bar," Martha called out, as if she were in another state.

"I think he heard that," Pru said.

"Good." Martha chuckled.

"Ruff!" Teddy added from the backseat.

Jesse started speaking again, and Pru nodded, even though she knew he couldn't see her.

"Okay, thanks. Sorry to bother you on a Sunday."

"What's he saying?" Martha asked.

"Yes, yoga is still on at the church hall on Tuesday. Okay. Bye."

"Well?" Martha asked impatiently when Pru ended the call.

"He asked at the bar about Bridget and no one admitted to seeing her in there. So it seems unlikely that she met Kevin there."

"Or that he had an off the books apartment or house to rent to her, I guess." Martha frowned. "Pooh." Then she brightened. "I caught the end of the call. Jesse's coming to your yoga on Tuesday." She sounded pleased.

"He said he'd try to make it. He's on call that evening."

"Make sure you wear your lipstick," Martha advised. "In case he's there. It's just as well we're gonna check out Bridget's room next, and see if we can pick up any clues."

Pru retrieved Martha's walker, and helped Teddy out of the car. Then they headed to the office.

"Hi, Martha," Paul, the owner, greeted them. Tall and lanky, he made the office seem super small. "Hi, Pru."

"This is Teddy," Martha introduced her fur baby.

"Ruff!" *Hi!*

"I've heard about Teddy." Paul smiled down at him. "Hi, boy."

"Ruff!

"What can I do for you?" He looked at them quizzically.

"We wanna check Bridget's room," Martha told him. "We're on a senior sleuthing club case."

"Why?" Paul furrowed his brow. "The police have already gone through it and told me I can re-rent it."

"Have you?" Pru asked.

"No. Not yet. I need to pack up Bridget's things and send them back to her folks in Colorado."

"They're not coming out here?" Pru asked. Her mother hadn't mentioned it.

"No." He shook his head. "They're busy planning the funeral and waiting for the bo – Bridget – to arrive."

"Then we've come just in time," Martha pronounced. "We might find a clue the police have missed."

"Why not?" Paul shrugged, then turned and took a brass key off the wall hook. "It's room nine on the ground floor."

"What else can you tell us about Bridget?" Martha asked.

"She seemed a nice enough girl, and paid on time – in fact, I make sure of that with all my guests." He tapped the card machine on the counter. "After being burned a few times years ago with allowing folks to pay when they checked out, now everyone needs to pay upfront, either cash or card. No exceptions."

"That's fair." Martha nodded.

"Unfortunately, some people aren't as trustworthy as they appear." Paul handed over the key.

"Thank you," Pru said.

"Bring it back when you're finished."

"We will," Martha replied.

"Ruff!"

They walked to room nine. Pru unlocked the door and taking a deep breath, pushed it open.

"This room isn't bad," Martha pronounced. "Apart from all of Bridget's stuff."

Pru eyed the scuffed blue suitcase lying on the floor. A book about California was on the small table as well as a heavy brass lamp. Jeans and T-shirts were strewn over the bed.

"I wonder if the police chucked those clothes there, or if they were already like that when they searched the place," Martha mused.

"Bridget wasn't always the tidiest person." Pru thought back to her college days.

"Now, after what Paul said about making sure all his guests paid upfront, I don't think he killed Bridget," Martha stated.

"No," Pru agreed.

"Ruff!" Teddy had been sniffing around, and now he scratched the hard suitcase with his front paws.

Pru stared at the case, then blinked. What if …

"Thanks, Teddy." She kneeled down and opened it. Luckily, it hadn't been locked.

"Whatcha doing?" Martha peered over her shoulder.

"Bridget had this suitcase in college and showed me a hidden compartment in here." Her voice was muffled as she rifled through an assortment of clothing to get to the bottom of the case.

"A zipper!" Martha sounded delighted.

"Wait." She unzipped the compartment and felt around. Nothing. But … it felt like something was underneath the lining. She smiled. "This is the real hidden compartment." Feeling inside the first section, she found the secret zip and pulled, making a metallic ripping noise. She gingerly inserted her fingers and encountered paper. Pulling a sheet out of the concealed section, she showed it to Martha and Teddy.

Her eyes widened when she realized what it was.

"That's you." Martha pointed to her photo on the black and white print out.

"Yes." It was a page from the library website, announcing Pru's appointment as assistant librarian.

"Huh. So she was what – stalking you?"

"She said someone told her mom where I was working before she left Colorado," Pru said. "I didn't make a big deal about moving here. I just packed my bags and left, after what happened at college."

"And she followed you here when she realized she couldn't get a job back home," Martha surmised. "And then she tried to get you to give her a job at the library."

"As if I could do that." Pru shook her head.

"Wuff." Teddy pawed at the hidden compartment with his fluffy white paw.

"Is there something else in there?" Pru stuck her hand in again and felt around. Paper brushed against her fingertip and she pulled it out gently.

"It's a scrap of white paper," Martha observed.

"With what looks to be a cell phone number on it." She stared at the numbers. "It's not my number." She showed it to Martha.

"I don't think that's mine." Martha frowned. "Maybe you should dial it and see if my phone rings. Just to make sure."

"Okay." Pru pulled her phone out of her purse and dialed. Martha's phone stayed silent.

"Is your phone on?"

"Of course it's on – wait, lemme check." Martha rummaged around in her walker basket. "Yeah – it's on, and I've got a signal!"

"It's going to voice mail," Pru said. "And it doesn't say whose number it is."

"Another mystery for the senior sleuthing club," Martha said in delight. "This might hold the key to solving Bridget's murder. Maybe Sunny's, too. Ooh – what if it's Angela's phone number?"

"Angela from the Sacramento yoga class?"

"Yep."

"I don't think this is the number you called when you booked us in to her class."

"Maybe this is her personal number."

"It could be," Pru replied. But why on earth would Bridget have Angela's phone number hidden in her suitcase?"

"You'd better put the scrap of paper in a safe place," Martha directed.

"Back in her suitcase?"

"I've been thinking." Martha tapped her head. "Paul said the police have been through everything here and he's allowed to pack all of Bridget's belongings and send them back to Colorado. So—"

"So?" Pru asked suspiciously.

"So what if we keep that piece of paper for ourselves? As part of the investigation?"

"But Martha—" she stared at her friend. "What if the police missed this?"

"Huh." Martha screwed up her face in thought. "I know! We can write down the number for ourselves and put the original back in the suitcase where you found it."

"Or we could take it to the police."

"So you can see Jesse – now you're thinking." Martha chuckled.

"No. Because it's the right thing to do."

"Of course it is. That's why you're a good girl. So you can keep me on my toes and help me be good, too. Okay. But only if we write down the number for ourselves first."

"Deal." Pru opened her purse and found a small notepad and pen. After carefully writing down the phone number, she glanced at Martha. "Should we look anywhere else in here?"

"You betcha. We haven't checked the bedside table or the wardrobe. Or under the mattress."

Pru heaved up the mattress but there was nothing underneath it, only wooden slats from the bedframe.

"Pooh." Martha was disappointed.

Pru opened the two drawers in the bedside table but apart from a Bible in the bottom drawer, they were empty.

"I'll check the wardrobe." Martha pulled open the wooden door, but only a couple of minidresses hung in there. "It seems like the clue is the phone number you found. I can't see anything else in here that would help our case."

"What about the bathroom?"

"Let's go!" Martha wheeled the few steps to the small bathroom which housed a commode, shower, and basin. "Apart from this fancy looking shampoo and her toothpaste and toothbrush, there's nothing else in here. Only an itty-bitty bit of soap."

"Paul provides small bars like that," Pru remembered.

"Well, it looks like we've finished." Martha looked around the bathroom in disappointment. "When my retired lady detective looks for clues, she finds more stuff than we did."

"We'd better return the key to Paul," she said, stifling a smile.

"And then stop by the police station on the way home," Martha added. "Wait until we tell Mitch or Jesse that they missed a clue!"

CHAPTER 16

To Martha's disappointment neither Mitch nor Jesse were at the police station.

"What do you mean, they're not here?" Martha asked the young, bored looking officer who picked at his thumbnail.

"What I said, lady – I mean ma'am. Detective Denman is out on a case and the new detective is having a day off. We *are* allowed time off, you know." He sounded as if he wished he was having a day off and resented being there.

"Can we leave something for them?" Pru asked.

"Yeah, it might be an important clue!" Martha told him.

The young officer looked like he wanted to guffaw at that, but refrained. "Sure. Give it to me."

Martha handed over the piece of paper with the cell phone number on it.

"Ruff?" Teddy stared up at the officer behind the counter.

"That's right." Pru nodded. "Could we get a receipt for it please?"

"Sure." He grabbed a notebook and scribbled in it. "Here you go."

"It doesn't look very official." Pru took the receipt from him and frowned at it. She showed it to Martha.

"You gotta put on it that we found it in Bridget's suitcase at the motel – room nine," Martha said importantly. "Not just 'piece of paper handed in by two ladies and a dog'".

"This should have the date on it as well," Pru pointed out.

"What are you two – amateur sleuths?" The officer stopped picking at his fingernail and leaned forward, a disgruntled expression on his face.

"Yeah, we are," Martha informed him. "I'm president of the senior sleuthing club and we've solved two murders so far. And right now we're on the trail of two more killers. Or maybe the same person killed Sunny and Bridget."

"I've never heard of this club," he said dismissively. "I'll give your piece of paper to the detectives. Don't worry about it. I'll even put it in a baggie." He opened the desk drawer, took out a small plastic bag, and placed the scrap of paper in it. "Satisfied?"

"It looks like we'll have to be," Pru replied.

"I'll make sure this gets to them," he repeated.

"Okay." Martha nodded. "I can always call Mitch tomorrow and check he received it. I've got his number on speed dial, you know."

The officer's eyes widened slightly. "Okay, okay," he grumbled. The desk phone rang and he answered it. "Gold Leaf Valley Police Department."

"Let's go home," Pru said.

"Ruff!"

"Yeah, I don't think he's going to help us anymore." Martha frowned at the officer who turned away from them and concentrated on the phone call.

Pru drove them home, hoping the officer kept his word and gave Mitch or Jesse the phone number they'd found.

"I've gotta work on my retired lady detective," Martha announced when they entered the house. "What are you going to do?"

"Teddy and I could play in the yard." She smiled down at him.

"Ruff!" *Yes!*

"Thanks. If I concentrate, I might finally finish this script tonight – with all the typos fixed up!"

"That would be great. I'd love to read it when you're done."

"You're the first," Martha promised. "Apart from my agent, of course. She wants the rest of it right away!"

"Of course." Pru nodded.

She played with Teddy in the yard for a while, throwing the ball, and AJ's soft mouse for him, enjoying watching him romp back to her with either item in his mouth, and throwing them again for him. After half an hour or so, they both tired, and went inside, where they sat together on the sofa. Pru picked up her Agatha Christie but couldn't concentrate. She couldn't help wondering if the young police officer was going to keep his word and give the scrap of paper continuing the phone number to Mitch or Jesse.

***

The next morning, Pru got up a little late and rushed through her shower and breakfast.

"I'm gonna send my script to my agent this morning." Martha munched on raisin toast at the table, looking a little bleary-eyed. "I've finally finished that darned script, and I've gotta admit, it's pretty good."

"I'm glad." Pru ate the last spoonful of her fiber rich but tasteless cereal before rinsing the bowl quickly. "I've got to go or I'll be late."

"Yeah, you don't want to get in trouble with Barb – I mean Barbara."

"That's right." She shot Martha a rueful glance.

After saying goodbye to Teddy and promising to play with him when she got home that afternoon, she dashed to her car and drove to the library, careful to observe the speed limit – barely.

Pru rushed into the library and glanced at the ticking clock on the wall. Made it with one minute to spare.

"Ah, Pru." Barbara suddenly appeared in front of her. How did she do that?

"Yes, Barbara?"

"I wanted to tell you I'm sorry about your friend. I heard about her demise."

"Thank you," she murmured.

"Even though she thought she was entitled to anything she wanted, it doesn't mean she should be killed like that. But I'm glad she's not around to drag you into a mess she might make. You're better than that, Pru. Make sure you remember that."

"Yes, Barbara. Thank you." She wasn't sure what else to say.

She watched her boss stride back to the reference desk, then Pru started scanning the returned books. She glanced over at the reference desk but Barbara's gaze was focused on the computer screen as she typed away. Did her comment mean she knew about the cheating scandal? Or was it because of the way Bridget had harangued her for a job?

She worked solidly all day, and was glad when the clock ticked four o'clock. Now she could go home and play with Teddy, and might even be able to start reading Martha's script, if she was allowed. And follow up whether the young police officer had given Mitch or Jesse the piece of paper with the phone number written on it.

***

"Ruff!" Teddy greeted her at the door with AJ's mouse in his mouth.

"Hello to you, too." She bent down to scratch him behind his ears, noticing his chin looked a little dirty. "What did you do today?"

"Ruff!" *Lots!*

"I sent the rest of the script to my agent!" Martha hollered down the hall.

"That's great."

Teddy romped ahead of her, and they entered the living room.

"Now you can read it." Martha thrust a sheaf of papers at her. "I printed it out for you."

"I'm looking forward to it." She took the bundle.

"And then I went to the senior center and came home and played with Teddy in the yard. He rolled around in the dirt and that's how he got his face dirty." Martha pointed to Teddy's chin. "Lucky he wasn't wearing one of his bandanas or I would have had to wash it."

"I can wash his chin for you," she offered.

"That would be good." Martha sounded relieved. "It's not so easy for me to bend down and do it."

After quickly getting the dirt off, Teddy and Pru returned to the living room.

"Did Mitch get the phone number from the officer at the station yesterday?" she asked.

"I've been thinking about that all day," Martha admitted. "And it's been bugging me, too. I'm gonna call him right now and find out." She pulled her phone out of her walker basket and dialed, getting Mitch straight away.

After a moment she said, "So he did give it to you? Uh-huh. Okay. Yeah. All right." Martha ended the call.

"Well?" Pru asked.

"Mitch said he got a bunch of papers when he came in this morning and he's still sorting through them because he went to Sacramento again to interview people in the Sunny case. So if he doesn't find it, he'll let us know."

"Good." She felt a little relieved. There had been something about the young police officer's attitude yesterday that she hadn't cared for.

"Now you can read about my retired lady detective." Martha looked at her expectantly.

"Ruff?" Teddy pawed at her knee. "Ruff! Ruff!"

"Uh oh. That's his *I wanna play* bark," Martha said.

"I did promise him this morning," Pru replied.

"You gotta keep your promises," Martha agreed.

"We'll play, and then I'll read your script," she said. "I've been looking forward to it."

"Goody." Martha sounded delighted.

After thirty minutes of throwing the mouse for Teddy, Pru was ready to relax on the sofa with the script. Teddy seemed to have the same idea, because he trotted back inside without a murmur and made himself comfy on the couch. Pru sank down beside him.

"I'll keep the sound off," Martha said, pointing to her game show on

TV. "You know how I sent away to be on that program? Well, I still haven't heard anything." She pouted.

"Maybe it takes them months to get back to you," Pru said. "They might get thousands of applicants each week."

"That could be true," Martha conceded. "Anyway, I've got my retired lady to keep me busy. My agent said she'll try and get back to me this week about it."

Pru began reading the script, impressed at its quality. Martha might moan about those pesky typos, but so far she hadn't encountered one. Her roommate was certainly full of surprises.

By dinner time, Pru had almost finished reading.

"Maybe I should do a speed-reading course," Martha mused. "You're so fast."

"You've got to keep up the practice otherwise you'll return to your normal reading speed," she cautioned.

"That's a poop."

"It is," she agreed. At times it was inconvenient to practice every day – or nearly every day, but overall it was worth it.

"Well?" Martha asked eagerly. "Do you like it? Did you read the part where the retired lady scares those two not so hotshots in the cemetery?"

"I did. I liked that."

"Goody. And what about the part where she gets stuck on a deserted road?"

"That was good, too."

"And what about—"

With all of Martha's interruptions, it took her longer than she expected to finish reading it.

"Well?" Martha asked again when she read the last page.

"I loved it!"

"Goody!" Martha looked delighted. "I hope my agent says she does, too. So far she said she liked it, but she hasn't read all of it like you have – yet."

They had beef casserole for dinner, and then settled down to watch a crime show.

"Huh," Martha said halfway through. "Maybe one day we'll find a dead body rolled up in a carpet."

"I hope not." She shivered.

When the show ended with the bad guy in jail, they said goodnight. Teddy trotted toward Martha's bedroom.

"It's your yoga class tomorrow," Martha said. "I can't wait!"

CHAPTER 17

Pru thought about her upcoming yoga class all Tuesday. Even the tasks she loved doing at the library, such as shelving books and making sure they were all in order and neatly arranged, didn't hold her interest as much. Would Jesse be there tonight? Would everyone turn up from her class last week? Would Angela, the yoga instructor from Sacramento, attend? Probably not – why would she be interested in Pru's beginner class, when Pru was just trying out teaching? She wasn't even qualified – not yet, anyway.

If Jesse turned up – would he treat her any differently now he knew about her cheating scandal? Nothing seemed off about his reaction to her calling him on Sunday about Bridget visiting the local bar, but that was a short conversation. She guessed she'd find out tonight – if he attended.

Luckily, she concentrated enough on her work not to draw Barbara's attention. When it was finally time to finish her shift, she felt relieved. Now all she had to do was don her yoga outfit and head to the church hall. She'd skip dinner, just like she had last week. She could eat after.

"Ready for yoga?" Martha appeared in the hall when she arrived home.

"Ruff!"

Pru blinked. "What are you – both of you – wearing?"

"Do you like it?" Martha turned around slowly, keeping a hand on her rolling walker and gesturing to her scarlet headband with the other.

"Teddy has one, too." Pru bent down to inspect the Coton's matching headband. "You look cute, Teddy – a bit like a pirate."

"Yeah, that's what I thought – but he's supposed to look like a yoga master – or is it yogi? We thought we'd jazz it up a bit for your class tonight and I had some red fabric left over from Teddy's bandanas."

"But he's not wearing a bandana."

"Not yet." Martha chuckled.

"Are you going to wear a red outfit as well?" She eyed Martha's turquoise sweatpants and matching top.

"No." Martha blew out a sigh. "I haven't got one that matches this." She pointed to the fabric tied around her springy gray curls. "We made you one, too." She rummaged around in her walker basket and pulled out a slightly crumpled piece of cloth.

"Thanks." Pru started tying it around her head.

"It might be a bit raggedy because I just cut the material, I didn't sew seams or anything," Martha apologized. "I just wanted to get it done."

"I understand."

"Ruff!"

"Now we're all matching!" Martha beamed.

A short while later, Pru changed into her yoga outfit. "Are you ready?"

"I think I was born ready." Martha chuckled.

"Ruff!" *Me too! And I'm wearing my bandana now!*

They got into Pru's silver SUV and drove the short distance to the church hall, the sky orange from the sun, which hadn't set yet.

"First again," Martha observed. "Park the closest to the hall."

"I was going to," she replied mildly.

"I thought I'd do at least floaty arms again tonight," Martha glanced at her hopefully. "You are doing that, aren't you?"

"Yes, but I'm going to try some different things as well."

"That's a good idea – change it up." Martha sounded approving.

She unlocked the hall, and rolled out her yoga mat.

"Teddy can take the money again," Martha said.

"That did work out well." She smiled at him.

"Ruff!" Teddy sniffed the wooden floorboards, taking extra care with the corners of the room.

"Maybe Annie taught him how to do that," Martha mused.

"I hope everyone comes." Pru went to the doorway and looked out, perking up when a white compact car drove up and parked next to her SUV. "It's Lauren and Zoe."

"Goody!" Martha sounded delighted. "Wait until I tell Zoe I've finished my retired lady script. I didn't go to the café today because I was a bit pooped from yesterday."

She greeted her friends, then was delighted when Doris, Brooke, and Claire turned up again. Everyone complimented them on the trio's matching headbands, and said how cute Teddy looked in his scarlet bandana as well.

Soon all of them were chatting, first about Martha's script, then about general topics. Teddy visited everyone and wriggled in delight at all the attention he received.

"I guess we'd better get started." Pru cleared her throat. It was just past the hour, but Jesse wasn't here. Not yet, anyway.

"You have to pay Teddy first," Martha declared.

"That's right." Zoe grinned.

"Ruff!"

Teddy took the payments, just like he had last week.

Pru was relieved that the two ladies she didn't know from last week hadn't turned up. Neither had Danielle. She wondered if the yoga enthusiast would arrive – or maybe Judith hadn't had a chance to tell Danielle's grandmother about tonight, after all.

"Sorry I'm late."

Her pulse fluttered when she heard Jesse's voice. She glanced over at the door, appreciating how he looked in the same outfit as last week – black shorts and a white T-shirt.

"Teddy's taking the money," Martha told him.

"Hi," she said shyly.

"Hi." He looked at her and smiled slightly.

While Jesse paid, Martha sidled up to her. "I don't think Danielle is coming."

"Me neither."

"Which is a poop for sure. I thought Judith would have given the girl's grandma the message about your class."

"Maybe Danielle's just not interested."

Martha blew out a gusty sigh. "I guess that means we'll have to track her down next week so we can ask her some questions about Sunny. And if we have to go to Sacramento to see Danielle, then we can pop in on Angela and ask her some follow up questions."

"Like what?"

"I'll think of something." Martha grinned.

Everyone took their places on their mats. The hall was wide enough for there to be one front row.

Jesse caught her eye. "I'm on call so I'll have to leave if my phone goes off."

"I understand." She nodded.

After taking them through the beginning movements, including floaty arms, which Martha did with gusto from her seated position on her walker, Pru moved them into the warrior poses.

"Watch out killers, here I come!" Martha sat on her walker and did the arm movements as best she could.

"Ruff!" Teddy agreed from his spot next to Pru.

Everyone started laughing, including Jesse. She exchanged a smile with him, realizing that so far he hadn't treated her any differently tonight even though he knew about her cheating scandal. Relief trickled through her, before she focused on the class and the rest of the postures she had in mind.

Halfway through the class, a loud buzz startled everyone.

"Sorry." Jesse reached into his bag and checked his phone. "I've got to go."

"Come back next week," Martha called.

Pru shot her a startled glance. Was there going to be a next week?

Jesse waved in acknowledgment and strode out of the hall.

"Let's try sphinx, everyone," Pru encouraged.

During the five-minute relaxation at the end, in corpse pose, she wondered if she should hold another class next week. Would everyone attend again? Would Jesse? It was a shame Danielle hadn't turned up, though. So far the senior sleuthing club hadn't done much cracking of cases this time.

"Are you teaching another class next week?" Brooke asked her when everyone gathered their things.

"I hadn't thought that far—"

"Yes, she is," Martha jumped in, then paused. "If she wants to."

"I hope you do," Claire said. "I love having a bit of time just for me and I really like your type of yoga, Pru."

"Thanks." She smiled.

"I think I'm getting better already," Doris said.

"Yeah, as long as you don't include too many downward dogs," Zoe joked.

"Okay, then," Pru found herself saying. "Same time next week?"

"I'll be here," Lauren told her. "Maybe Annie can come, too."

"Ruff!" *Yeah!*

Everyone looked hopefully at Pru.

"Of course." She smiled. "It will be fun."

"Awesome!" Zoe grinned.

Everyone said goodbye and headed out of the hall. Car engines started up, the sound fading as everyone drove home.

"Whatcha going to do with all the money?" Martha eyed the pile of cash.

"Give it to Father Mike. Maybe I can make this a weekly thing, if everyone's interested," she said slowly.

"I think they are." Martha nodded.

"Ruff!" *Yes!*

"And Doris seems to be enjoying herself," Pru said.

"I am, too," Martha chuckled. "Did you see me doing the floaty arms again? I—"

"Is this Pru's yoga?" Danielle suddenly appeared in the doorway.

She looked at Danielle in surprise. "It was, but—"

"We've finished," Martha said cheerfully. "We hoped you'd come but we had to get started."

"It's supposed to start at eight." Danielle frowned.

"No, seven o'clock." Pru replied.

"Are you serious?" Danielle placed her hands on her hips. "My grandma's friend told me it started at eight and here I am. I wanted to see exactly what you did wrong so I could correct you."

"What about that hot yoga class you took last week?" Pru asked.

"That was terrible." Danielle made a face. "She wasn't nearly as good an instructor as Sunny. I don't know what I'm going to do, and there are plenty of us that feel the same way. We need a yoga teacher like Sunny!"

"Maybe *you* could be that teacher," Pru told her.

"Once I get my qualification I can," Danielle remarked. "Like I told Sunny, I'm on the waitlist for that yoga school. It's the best one around, and if you want to be the best, then you need to study from the best. Don't you agree?"

"I wouldn't know with regard to yoga, since I don't have a teaching certification."

"But Pru's a big enthusiast, which counts for a lot," Martha told her. "Everyone tonight loved her class and she's gonna teach it again next week. At seven."

Teddy sniffed Danielle's sneakers, then walked around her and inspected her pink and white polka dot socks.

"What's he doing?" Danielle frowned down at him.

"Checking you out," Martha told her. "See if he wants to be friends with you."

"Ruff!" Teddy trotted over to Martha and Pru.

"It looks like he doesn't want to be pals," Martha told her. "Sorry." She didn't sound it.

"As if I care." Danielle sniffed. "I can't believe I drove a whole hour just to get here and check out your class, and it's over."

"I'm sorry," Pru said.

"Your friends didn't come tonight," Martha commented. "They were your friends, weren't they? The two ladies we didn't know who came last week?"

"Yeah, they were," Danielle replied. "But they said it was too focused on boring beginner stuff and they felt like they wasted their time – and money."

Since Pru had already apologized, even though it hadn't been her fault that Danielle had missed the class, she didn't feel like apologizing again right now.

"You gotta start somewhere," Martha said. "See, even though I can't do all the moves, Pru's class is just right for me."

Now Danielle was here, it was the perfect time to ask her some questions about Sunny's murder. But where should they start? Pru glanced at Martha, who was still telling

Danielle how great the class was tonight.

"Did you see anyone suspicious hanging around the night Sunny died?" Pru asked. "It was after her yoga class here."

"Not here here, though," Martha put in. "But in that upstairs studio on the main street."

"No. Why would I?" Danielle frowned.

"Because if I remember correctly, you were still there when I left. I thought you might have heard or seen something strange."

"Yeah. Something that will lead us to Sunny's killer!" Martha said enthusiastically.

"Ruff!" Teddy darted forward and sniffed Danielle's sneakers again.

"What are you doing?" Danielle lifted one foot and then the other, as Teddy wouldn't be deterred.

"You must have an interesting smell on your shoes," Martha said.

"Ruff!" Teddy grabbed hold of a shoelace and tugged.

"Stop that!" Danielle stepped back. "Make him stop! I bought those laces specially for these sneakers."

Pru admired the pristine white sneakers and laces, but wondered how practical that color was.

"Teddy, stop doing that," Martha scolded.

"Wuff." Teddy dropped the shoelace in disappointment and trotted slowly back to Martha.

"Good boy," Pru praised.

"Yeah, it's real good that you stopped doing that when I asked you to," Martha also complimented him.

"Ruff!" Teddy scampered over to Danielle again and sniffed the side of her sneaker.

"Teddy," Martha said. "She doesn't want you doing that. What are you—"

"Wait," Pru said slowly. From her vantage point, she was able to see the part of the sneaker Teddy was interested in. If she squinted, she could see a faint scratch along the side. Sunny was killed by trip wire placed on the stairs. What if that scratch was caused by the trip wire?

"Teddy, you'd better come back here," Martha told him.

Teddy glanced at Pru, who nodded at him, trying to tell him she'd noticed the scratch on the sneakers. When he returned to Martha, she pulled out the phone from her purse and the notepad where she'd written the mysterious phone number, and dialed, aware of Martha's curious gaze.

A snatch of music trilled in the hall. Danielle's eyes widened. "That's my phone!" She rummaged through her tote bag and answered. "Hello?"

"It's Pru." She spoke into her cell, staring directly at Danielle.

"What are you …" Danielle's voice trailed off.

"Ah-ha!" Martha pointed at her. "Bridget had your phone number for some reason!"

"Bridget?" Sunny furrowed her brow, but she'd paled. "I don't know a Bridget."

"She was at Sunny's class here in Gold Leaf Valley," Pru informed her.

"Why would she have your number?" Martha asked. "She told Pru she was just passing through, until she hit up Pru for a job in the library. You don't work in a library, do you?"

"No, I don't work at all." Danielle sounded smug. "Because I don't need to. Unless it's to become a yoga teacher."

"I left Sunny's class before you," Pru said slowly.

"So?" Danielle shrugged, but it didn't seem as insouciant as she might have intended. "I wanted to talk to Sunny after class, and get some advice about when I start my teaching training. I don't know who this Bridget girl is at all."

"She was killed in the local park," Pru said.

"Yeah, someone smashed a rock over her head," Martha added.

"Ruff!" Teddy ran back to Danielle and sniffed the side of her sneaker again, then tapped it with his paw.

"Thanks, Teddy." Pru smiled at him, although her heart pounded.

"What's that scratch on your sneaker, Danielle? Do you think it could be caused by trip wire? The same trip wire that was used to kill Sunny on the stairs?"

"What?" Danielle took a step back. "I have no idea what you're talking about!"

"But I – we – think you do." Martha inched toward her with the walker. "Bridget had your phone number for some reason, and you've got a suspicious scratch on your sneaker. Now's the time to come clean."

"You're crazy!" Danielle shook her head.

"I'll call Jesse," Pru said. "I'm sure he'll be very interested to find out Bridget had your phone number."

"Yeah, we found it in her suitcase, hidden in a secret compartment," Martha added. "Why would Bridget put it in there unless it was important?"

"How would I know?" Danielle snapped. "I'm leaving now. How dare you accuse me?" She turned on her heel and promptly fell over. "Ow!"

Pru's eyes widened as she saw the untied shoelace on Danielle's sneaker.

"Ruff!" Teddy sounded proud of himself.

"I'm sorry." Pru knelt to help her up. "I didn't realize Teddy had actually untied your shoelace."

"I'm going to sue!" A tear rolled down Danielle's cheek. "You don't realize how stressful all this is! Sunny's gone!"

"If you didn't kill her, how can you explain the scratch on your sneaker?" Martha wanted to know.

"I don't know! I wear these sneakers all the time to yoga. Maybe someone bumped me with the buckle on their shoe when I was coming into class and I didn't notice. Or maybe someone deliberately scratched my sneaker. We do take them off at the start of the class and line them up in a corner of the room, you know. Somone could have been jealous of them and decided to ruin them."

"Or you could have scratched them yourself when you laid the tripwire on the stairs for Sunny to fall over," Martha declared.

Teddy nosed around Danielle's shoes while Pru tried to help her up.

"I'm going home now and I don't want you bothering me again! Otherwise I'll sic my lawyer onto you!" Danielle got to her feet, pushing away Pru's helping hand. "I can get up by myself. I'm super limber from yoga." Taking a couple of steps forward and picking up her yoga mat, she stumbled and tripped again, sprawling on the ground.

"Ow!"

"Teddy!" Pru scolded.

"Ruff!" Teddy ran around Danielle. "Ruff! Ruff!"

"I think he's saying she's the killer," Martha said. "Teddy doesn't untie my shoelaces."

"Nor mine," Pru replied.

"My ankle!" Danielle clutched her left ankle. "I think it's broken!"

"It might only be a sprain." Pru knelt down again to take a look. "May I touch it?"

"No! Keep your hands away from me!" Danielle wiggled her butt across the floorboards, towards the door. "I'm getting out of here!"

"Ruff!" Teddy raced to the door and stood in front of it. Although he was only nine inches tall, there was a determined glint in his eye.

"Out my way, dog!" Danielle crawled toward him. "Don't try to stop me or I'll—"

"You'll what?" Martha placed her hands on her hips. "You've got a suspicious scratch on your shoe and Bridget had your phone number. If you weren't up to something shady with her, you wouldn't have a problem telling us why she had your number. So that leaves us with only one conclusion. You're the killer! And you killed both Sunny *and* Bridget!"

"Ruff!" *Yeah!* Teddy still barred the exit.

"Okay, fine," Danielle sobbed, still on her hands and knees. "I did it! Are you happy now?"

"No, I'm not happy you killed two people," Pru said.

"Yeah, why did you do it?" Martha asked.

"It's all Sunny's fault! I loved her so much – as a teacher, you know? Not the other way. But she was mean to me. I was her greatest fan. I wanted to talk to her after class about training to be a teacher and get some more advice from her, but she was in a foul mood, ranting about Kevin wanting her to pay all the rent, and what was she supposed to do about that? And then she turned on me, telling me I'll never be a great teacher like her because I can't commit to teacher training, and to stop wasting her time!" Danielle gulped. "How did she think she got half her students? Because I went around telling everyone how great Sunny was and they should try her yoga class!

And then," Danielle took in a big, heaving sob, "she told me not to come to her class again! That she didn't want me anywhere near her!"

"I'm sorry," Pru said, feeling helpless.

"Yeah, that's real mean," Martha added.

"Ruff," Teddy said sadly.

"So I snapped! How dare Sunny talk to me like that? She'll never have someone who looked up to her like I did. So I ran out of the studio, and saw a thin piece of wire lying on the floor outside. I have no idea what it was doing there, but I bent down and grabbed it, and that's when it must have scratched the side of my sneaker, but I didn't realize. Then I tied the wire around the bottom of the handrails on each side of the staircase, right up the top. I was the last to leave – do you think Sunny would have spoken to me like that in front of everyone? – so I knew the wire would only hurt Sunny and no one else. But I didn't think it would *kill* her! I thought she might just break her leg or something." She turned a tear-stained face up to them in appeal.

"What about Bridget?" Pru asked.

"Oh, her." Danielle shook her head, her expressing darkening. "It served her right. What a nosy parker. And she tried to blackmail me!"

"Really?" Martha asked.

"Yeah, she forgot something and came back to the studio for it – or so she said later on – and overheard Sunny being mean to me. And then after Sunny's death was reported in the media, she tracked me down in Sacramento at Angela's yoga studio where I was searching for a new yoga instructor. Who does that? And said she'd go to the police and tell them what she'd overheard, unless I paid her not to."

Pru's mouth parted. Surely this was a new low for Bridget?

"So I gave her my phone number and she called to arrange a time to meet so I could give her five hundred dollars."

"And when you met her in the park you killed her," Martha guessed.

"Yeah. Everyone knows blackmailers don't stop. And she'd be able to find out that my family is wealthy and we have plenty of money, if she hadn't done that already. She would have kept coming back and coming back asking for more and more until I'd have to explain to my dad why I'd gone through my monthly allowance so fast. He's told me before I need to manage my money better or else he'll make me go get a *job*!" She made it sound like the worst thing in the world.

"So no way was I going to let Bridget do that to me. And you know what she said when I turned up to meet her? The first words out of her mouth were, 'You can meet me here again next week with another five hundred.'

"So when she was busy counting the money, her back was turned. I saw a rock, grabbed it, and hit her over the head with it. Then I wiped my fingerprints off the rock with my sweater, picked up the money and ran."

"You were lucky no one saw you," Pru observed.

"Yeah. The park was deserted. Maybe she'd already scoped it out so no one would see us."

"I guess it's true what they say – cheaters never prosper – and neither do blackmailers," Martha stated.

"Yes," Pru murmured, feeling sick.

"So what are you going to do now?" Danielle challenged. "Nobody knows what I did – except you two—" she glanced at Teddy "—three."

"We're – we're—" Martha looked around wildly, her gaze settling on Pru's forehead. "We're going to tie you up and call the police!"

"With what?" Danielle scoffed, inching once more toward the door, despite Teddy guarding it.

"With this!" With a flourish, Martha yanked off Pru's red headband.

"Ouch!" Pru rubbed her forehead.

"Sorry, but this is an emergency!" Martha advanced toward Danielle with her walker.

"I don't think Danielle is going anywhere." She gestured to the girl on her hands and knees.

"It might be a trick," Martha declared. "She might not have hurt her ankle at all. If we relax our guard, she might spring up and attack us!"

"You got that right!" Danielle leaped to her feet, stumbling on her ankle.

Pru rushed toward Martha, but the rolling walker and Teddy halted Danielle's bid for freedom.

"Ruff! Ruff, ruff!" Teddy barked non-stop, running back and forth across the open doorway.

"One more move and I'll ram you in the back of your legs with my walker," Martha warned. "Then you'll fall down."

"No I won't." Danielle sprinted towards Teddy. "Ow!" She tumbled onto the wooden floorboards, and clutched her ankle.

"Told you," Martha said, looming over her. She patted the walker. "This thing is very reliable."

"We'd better call Jesse and Mitch." Pru started dialing.

"Not before we tie her up. Just to be sure."

"Okay." She'd genuinely thought Danielle had injured her ankle, but it couldn't be as bad as she'd made out if she'd been able to get up so quickly to make a dash for it.

Pru tied Danielle's hands in the front, making sure she didn't make the knot too tight.

"I can't believe you're doing this," Danielle wailed. "You're – you're – kidnapping me!"

"No, we're not. We're just making sure you don't move until the police arrive," Martha explained.

Pru called Jesse and explained the situation.

"He said someone will be here ASAP, but he's attending a burglary right now. It will be either him or Mitch."

"Goody." Martha nodded. "Just wait until we tell them that we've caught a double killer. We might even get a medal!'

"Ruff!"

EPILOGUE

Later that evening, Jesse came to the house. Pru had just been about to change into her pajamas, but now she was glad she hadn't.

"Well?" Martha asked eagerly, ushering Jesse into the living room.

"Ruff?" Teddy scampered ahead of him, leading the way.

"Hi," she said, rising from the sofa.

"Hi." Jesse looked tired, and his hair was slightly rumpled. He was in his work clothes of dark slacks and a gray shirt.

When Jesse had arrived at the church hall and had taken Danielle into custody, he told them to go home and he'd come over later that night to take their statements.

"How is Danielle's ankle?" Pru asked.

"The paramedics say it's a minor sprain. She should be fine."

"Good," she replied.

"Is she gonna go to jail?" Martha asked. "She should, considering she killed two people."

"Yes, she should," Jesse agreed. "But as soon as we took her to the police station she asked to call her lawyer – who's a very high-priced one. But with your testimony, and the evidence you found in Bridget's suitcase – Danielle's phone number – we're confident we can put her away."

"Did Mitch receive the scrap of paper we found in Bridget's suitcase?" Pru asked. When Jesse had arrived at the church hall, they'd quickly told him how they'd found Danielle's phone number in the motel room and called the number during their confrontation with Danielle.

"He hadn't realized you'd dropped it off," he replied. "He's torn a strip off the desk officer, who just bundled it up with some other papers and gave them to Mitch, and didn't tell him you'd brought it in personally and where you found it. I think that guy will be looking for a new job."

"Good." It seemed her instinct had been right about that young police officer.

"Yeah!" Martha added. "He just didn't take us seriously."

"He's regretting that now." Jesse drew in a breath. "And I have to admit you caught the killer in both cases. Maybe the senior sleuthing club is on the right track at times."

"At times?" Martha stared at him. "How about all the time? We've caught the killer in every single case we've investigated."

"That doesn't mean you should keep doing it," Jesse replied. "It could get dangerous. Mitch or I might not always be around to stop you from getting hurt."

"We can stop ourselves from getting hurt," Martha told him. "Isn't that right, Pru? We tied up Danielle with Pru's headband, which I made."

"Ruff!" Teddy agreed.

"Yeah, and now Danielle's lawyer is talking about how you unlawfully restrained her. Don't worry, it's obvious it's bogus, and you tied the cloth pretty loosely around her hands. She could have probably broken free if she'd really wanted to." He shook his head. "Her lawyer is just trying it on. But that's what happens when civilians nab killers."

"Huh," Martha huffed. "You're welcome, anyway. Maybe one day me and Pru and Teddy will get real police badges because of all the murderers we've caught. Although by now, Lauren, Annie, and Zoe should already be wearing them."

Just then Martha's phone buzzed from her walker basket.

"Ooh – who's calling at this hour?"

Pru checked her watch. "It's nearly ten."

"Sorry I couldn't get here sooner," Jesse apologized.

"It's okay," she murmured. "You must be really busy with Danielle."

"Mitch is taking charge of that," he told her.

"Really?" Martha's voice cut through their conversation. "Uh-huh. Yeah. Goody! You betcha! Okay, talk to you soon!" Martha ended the call and turned to them, her face flushed, and grinning widely from ear to ear. "That was my agent. She's just finished reading the rest of the script about my retired lady detective and she's gonna send it to that TV producer who's looking for a new show. She loves it!"

"That's wonderful!" Pru smiled.

"Yeah, it is."

"Ruff!" *Yay!* Teddy gamboled around Martha's feet.

"So you're a writer as well as an amateur sleuth?" Jesse raised an eyebrow.

"Yeah, didn't Pru tell you? Maybe you two should spend more time together and get up to speed about some things. Well, if you don't need me, Jesse, I'm gonna go to bed now. It's been a long day."

"Of course." Jesse headed for the door.

"Pru, see him out, would you?"

She nodded. Martha was right – it *had* been a long day and she had to go to work tomorrow.

At the front door, Jesse paused and turned to face her.

"There was something else I wanted to tell you. When you told me about Bridget using you to cheat on her college exams, I knew there was no way you could be wittingly involved in something like that. You're one of the most principled people I've ever met." He smiled. "Maybe that's one of the reasons I like you."

"Thanks." She knew she was blushing, and there was nothing she could do to stop it. A weight she hadn't known she'd carried lifted off her heart.

They stared at each other for a long moment, then Jesse's phone buzzed. He dug it out of his pocket and checked the screen. "It's Mitch. He needs me back at the station."

"You'd better go."

Teddy charged up the hall toward them.

"He wants to say goodbye to Jesse," Martha hollered.

"See you soon, Teddy. And you, Pru." Jesse winked at both of them. "Ruff!"

THE END

If you sign up to my newsletter, you'll receive a Free and Exclusive short story titled **When Martha Met Her Match.** It's about Martha adopting Teddy from the animal shelter and takes place during **Prowling at the Premiere – A Norwegian Forest Cat Café Cozy Mystery – Book 23**, but it can also be read as a standalone, and it's also the first title in Martha's Senior Sleuthing Club series!

Sign up to my newsletter here: www.JintyJames.com
If you already receive my newsletter and didn't receive the short story, please email me at jinty@jintyjames.com and mention the email address you used to sign up with, and I'll send you the link.

TITLES BY JINTY JAMES

Book Clubs Can Be Fatal – A Senior Sleuthing Club Cozy Mystery – Book 1

Garage Sales Can Be Fatal – A Senior Sleuthing Club Cozy Mystery – Book 2

Norwegian Forest Cat Café Series:

Purrs and Peril – A Norwegian Forest Cat Café Cozy Mystery – Book 1

Meow Means Murder - A Norwegian Forest Cat Café Cozy Mystery – Book 2

Whiskers and Warrants - A Norwegian Forest Cat Café Cozy Mystery – Book 3

Two Tailed Trouble – A Norwegian Forest Cat Cafe Cozy Mystery – Book 4

Paws and Punishment – A Norwegian Forest Cat Café Cozy Mystery – Book 5

Kitty Cats and Crime – A Norwegian Forest Cat Café Cozy Mystery – Book 6

Catnaps and Clues - A Norwegian Forest Cat Café Cozy Mystery – Book 7

Pedigrees and Poison – A Norwegian Forest Cat Café Cozy Mystery – Book 8

Christmas Claws – A Norwegian Forest Cat Café Cozy Mystery – Book 9

Fur and Felons - A Norwegian Forest Cat Café Cozy Mystery – Book 10

Catmint and Crooks – A Norwegian Forest Cat Café Cozy Mystery – Book 11

Four-Footed Fortune – A Norwegian Forest Cat Café Cozy Mystery – Book 19

Rewards and Revenge – A Norwegian Forest Cat Café Cozy Mystery – Book 20

Catnip and Capture – A Norwegian Forest Cat Café Cozy Mystery – Book 21

Mice and Malice – A Norwegian Forest Cat Café Cozy Mystery – Book 22

Prowling at the Premiere – A Norwegian Forest Cat Café Cozy Mystery – Book 23

Maddie Goodwell Series (fun witch cozies)

Spells and Spiced Latte - A Coffee Witch Cozy Mystery - Maddie Goodwell 1

Visions and Vanilla Cappuccino - A Coffee Witch Cozy Mystery - Maddie Goodwell 2

Magic and Mocha – A Coffee Witch Cozy Mystery – Maddie Goodwell 3

Enchantments and Espresso – A Coffee Witch Cozy Mystery – Maddie Goodwell 4

Familiars and French Roast - A Coffee Witch Cozy Mystery – Maddie Goodwell 5

Incantations and Iced Coffee – A Coffee Witch Cozy Mystery – Maddie Goodwell 6